Enid Blyton's

Enchanted Tales

THE FARAWAY
TREE ADVENTURE

Enid Blyton's
Enchanted Tales

Enid Blyton's Enchanted Tales

THE FARAWAY TREE ADVENTURE

Illustrated by Gunvor Edwards

RED FOX

A Red Fox Book

Published by Random House Children's Books
20 Vauxhall Bridge Road, London SW1V 2SA

A division of The Random House Group Ltd
London Melbourne Sydney Auckland
Johannesburg and agencies throughout the world

Text copyright © Enid Blyton Limited, 1936
Illustrations copyright © Gunvor Edwards, 1993
Enid Blyton's signature is a registered
trademark of Enid Blyton Limited

1 3 5 7 9 10 8 6 4 2

First published as The Queer Adventure by Newnes 1936
Published as The Yellow Fairy Book by Red Fox 1993

Red Fox edition 2000

Printed and bound in Great Britain by
Cox and Wyman Ltd, Reading, Berkshire

THE RANDOM HOUSE GROUP Limited Reg. No. 954009

www.randomhouse.co.uk

ISBN 0 09 940804 X

Contents

CHAPTER ONE

The Little
Princess Fenella

This is the story of a strange adventure. It happened to two children, Peter and Mary. They were twins and lived with their father and mother in a small cottage.

Their home was in a most exciting place, for their cottage was just outside the gates of Fairyland. Their mother sometimes did washing for the little folk, and she was allowed to go shopping in the little village inside the golden gates.

The children loved to go with her. At first the fairies had not been very pleased to see a boy and girl in their village beyond the gates, but they soon liked them very much.

'Come and have tea with me,' said Fairy Tiptap. 'I'll give you lemonade cakes, a kind you've never had before!'

'Come and see my big black cat,' said the pixie

Tippitty. 'He keeps house for me. Nobody can sweep or dust better than he can!'

But the greatest excitement of all was when Lady Rozabel came clattering along in her

coach one day, and saw Peter and Mary. She liked the look of them so much that she stopped her coach at once and leaned out of the window.

'Who are these children? I want companions for my little girl, the Princess Fenella, and I think perhaps they are just the right age to be with her,' she said.

Out of the window peeped the small Princess. She had curly golden hair, eyes like forget-me-nots, and the naughtiest smile that ever was seen.

'Mother!' she said, when she saw Peter and Mary. 'I like these children. I want them to play with me!'

'If they come, they will have to work with you, too,' said the Lady Rozabel. 'Perhaps you will do your lessons better then!'

Peter and Mary went to tea with Fenella, and the Lady Rozabel thought what good manners they had, and how kind they were to naughty little Fenella. That was the beginning of a grand time for the two children!

Fenella had wonderful toys and loved to share them with Peter and Mary. They shared lessons too, and Fenella worked much harder than usual because she didn't want to be beaten by her two new friends.

After lessons they played in the garden. It was a most exciting place. There was a magic swing, which if you shut your eyes, would swing you to anywhere you wanted to go – but it was dangerous to get off the swing until you were home again, because you might be left behind in some strange place!

There was a little river where they sailed boats, and paddled and bathed. There was a tiny house just big enough for the three children to get inside and play housekeeping. There was a very high tree from which, if they climbed to the top, they could actually see the towers of Giantland, very far away.

And there was the Magic Well. The children were not allowed to go near this.

'Remember, children, never go near the Magic Well,' Lady Rozabel told them over and over again. 'Something dreadful will happen if you do.'

Now one day Fenella lost her favourite ball. The three children hunted everywhere but they couldn't find it. Fenella flung herself down on the grass, and wailed loudly.

'What's the matter with the little lady!' suddenly said a shrill voice. The children looked round in surprise, and saw a small gnome stooping over a stick, his long beard reaching to the grass. He had bright green eyes that shone strangely.

'I've lost my ball and can't find it,' said the Little Princess, staring at the strange fellow.

'Well – go to the Magic Well and wish for it!' said the gnome. 'Don't you know that you have only to bend over the well and whisper your wish for it to come true?'

'Really!' said all the children, excited. 'Well – let's go!'

'I'll show you the way,' said the gnome, and he hobbled along in front of them. He took them to a small glade, a dim and silent place where no bird sang, and no rabbit peeped. Peter felt uneasy and wanted to go back, but Fenella shook her curly head at once.

'I'm going to wish!' she said. 'I'm *not* going back till I've wished for my ball!'

'Let Mary wish first, or me,' said Peter. 'Just to see if it's all right, you know.'

'Well, make haste then,' said Fenella.

Peter bent over the deep well. The water seemed a long way down. Cold air came up from

11

it and he shivered. He knew what he wanted to wish. His mother was often ill – it would be lovely if she could always be well.

'I wish that my mother may never be ill again, but may always be well and strong,' he said firmly.

'That's a fine wish,' said Mary. 'Now *I'll* wish. I wish that my daddy will one day be rich and have a fine house!' she called down the well.

'That's a good idea too,' said Peter. 'Now, Fenella, wish for your ball.'

'No – first it is *my* turn,' said the gnome suddenly, in a strange voice. He pushed the children aside and leaned over the well. Peter was angry.

'No – it's Fenella's turn!' he said. 'How dare you be so rude to a princess!'

The gnome pushed Peter away roughly. Then he suddenly caught hold of Fenella and shouted loudly,

'I wish to be away, away, away!'

And, to the children's dreadful dismay, the gnome and Fenella vanished completely! Then there was a gurgling of water and the well vanished too! Nothing was left of it, not even a brick or a shining drop of water!

'Fenella's gone!' cried Peter, scared.

'Whatever are we to do?' said Mary, trembling. 'Call her, Peter.'

'Fenella! Fenella!' shouted Peter, looking all through the glade. But there was no one at all. Fenella had vanished with the gnome.

'I might have guessed he was up to mischief,' said Peter, miserably. 'He had such strange green eyes.'

'We'll have to tell the Lady Rozabel,' said Mary, tears running down her cheeks. So the two of them rushed to the palace with their bad news.

'Fenella's gone!' they cried. 'A gnome took her away, just by the Magic Well!'

At once there was a great upset. The gardens were searched from end to end. The well was hunted for, but, of course, it could not be found.

'You bad children!' raged Lord Rolland, Fenella's father. 'Weren't you told not to go near the well? Now the gnome Sly-One has got Fenella, and goodness knows what will happen. He may keep her prisoner – he may sell her for gold – he may even turn her into a black cat and keep her for a servant! I once turned him out of Fairyland and he vowed he would pay me out for that – now he has!'

'Go home!' said Lady Rozabel, weeping

13

bitterly. 'You should be beaten for letting Fenella go near the well. Go home – and never come back!'

The two children ran off at once, scared and miserable. Through the golden gates of Fairy-land they went and back to their cottage home.

They found their mother ill in bed. Their father was tending her, dressed in his rough shepherd clothes.

'Our wishes didn't come true,' said Peter, sadly. 'Mother is ill instead of well – and our father is still a poor shepherd, and not a rich man.'

'Oh Mother!' cried Mary, 'a dreadful thing has happened!' She sank down by her mother's bed and told her everything.

'This is a terrible thing,' said her mother. 'The poor Lady Rozabel – and poor little Fenella! Why, oh why did you let her go near that well! There is only one thing to do – you must go and find the little Princess!'

CHAPTER TWO

The Beginning of the Adventure

Peter and Mary stared at their mother in surprise. 'But Mother! We don't know where she is!' said Peter.

'I think I can guess,' said his mother. 'She will be with the gnome Sly-One, of course, and he will have taken her to his own land.'

'Where's that?' asked Peter, eagerly.

'Well, when the Lord Rolland turned him out of Fairyland, he went to the Land of Story-tellers,' said his mother. 'A very good place for such a sly rascal, too! I'm sure that is where he has taken the little princess.'

'But how do we get there?' asked Mary. 'I've never even heard of such a land, Mother.'

'I can tell you,' said her father. 'You must first find your way to the Land of the Stupids. It's a great pity to have to go there — you may find

15

it difficult to get away. Then from there you must travel through Giantland.'

'Oh dear – I don't like that,' said their mother. 'Try not to be seen there, my dears. You never know what may happen if the giants catch sight of two little people like you.'

'After Giantland you will come to the Land of Storytellers,' said their father. 'When you get there you must find out where the gnome Sly-One lives, and see if you can somehow rescue the Princess.'

'It all sounds very difficult and rather frightening,' said Mary, afraid.

'Don't worry, Mary, *I'll* look after you,' said Peter, squeezing her arm. 'It will be a great adventure with something worth winning at the end. If we never come back at least we shall have tried to do something. The thing is – which is the way to the Land of the Stupids?'

'I can help you, I think,' said their father. 'I will take you to the Enchanted Wood. In the middle of it is an enormous tree, the Faraway Tree.'

'Whatever kind of tree is that?' said Mary in surprise.'

'It's a strange tree,' said her father. 'All kinds of little folk live in it. At the top is a great branch that pierces through the clouds. A little yellow ladder leads up from the branch – and at the top you will find a strange land.'

'A land – at the top of a *tree*!' cried Peter. 'What land?'

'Well, a new land comes every week,' said his father. 'Sometimes it may be the Land of Spells, sometimes the Land of Secrets, sometimes Toyland, sometimes the Land of Birthdays. And soon the Land of Stupids will be there.'

'Oh!' cried Peter. 'So if we climb the Faraway Tree we may get to the Land of Stupids quite easily. How do you know all this, Father?'

'I have a cousin who lives in the tree,' said his father. 'A little fellow called Moonface. I meet him sometimes, when I am watching my sheep, and he gives me the news of the Faraway Tree, and tells me about the strange lands that come there. We will set off now. If we delay you may miss the Land of Stupids.'

'Take some food with you,' said their mother. 'And look – take this too. It may be of some use. It is the only precious thing I have.'

She held out to Peter a small round box rather like a pill-box. Peter took it and opened it. Inside was some purple powder as fine as flour.

'What is it for?' asked the boy, in surprise.

'You must wait and see,' said his mother. 'If you do not use it, bring it back. My old granny, who was half a fairy, gave it to me. It is rare and very valuable. If the right time comes, you will use it – but not until.'

'Come,' said their father. 'We must hurry, or night will be on us. It is a long way to the Enchanted Wood.'

'Goodbye, dears,' said their mother. 'There's nothing much more I can say to you, except to tell you to be brave and kind.'

'We promise to be,' said the twins, and kissed their mother. 'Goodbye! We'll find the Princess and bring her back – we'll do our very best!'

Off they went with their father. He took them over the fields to a big hill, and down the other side. They walked through valleys, and passed many villages, and at last they came to the Enchanted Wood.

The Faraway Tree was right in the middle. When the children came to it they stared in surprise. It was so enormous! They looked up and up, and saw that its topmost branches reached the clouds.

A little squirrel in a red jersey came bounding up. 'Sir,' he said to the children's father, 'I am sure I have seen you before. You are Mr Moonface's cousin! Shall I take you up to his little house in the top of the tree?'

'Thank you,' said everyone, and followed

the squirrel as he bounded up the tree. The children were surprised and delighted as they climbed. There were little windows and doors in the tree, and how they wished they could peep in at the windows and knock at the doors!

But there was no time. They mustn't miss the Land of the Stupids! At last they came to the top of the tree, and saw a little door there, set in the round trunk. The squirrel knocked and it opened.

A little man with a round, shining face and

twinkling eyes looked out. 'Why – if it's not Cousin John the shepherd!' he said. 'And his two children. Come along in!'

'Well – we don't know if we've time to stop,' said the children's father. 'My two children want to go to the Land of Stupids, and I believe it's about time it came to the top of the Faraway Tree, isn't it?'

'Yes, it comes tomorrow,' said Moonface. 'So do come in and stay the night. How nice to see you all!'

They all went into Moonface's little round room inside the tree. The furniture was curved to fit round the inside of the trunk. In the middle was a big hole.

'Don't go near it unless you want to find yourself at the bottom of the tree!' said Moonface. 'That's my slippery-slip – a short cut to the foot of the tree. It goes round and round and down and down all through the tree.'

The children thought it sounded very exciting and longed to try it. But they didn't because they were tired, and they knew they would have to climb all the way up the tree again if they found themselves at the bottom!

Moonface gave them a lovely supper, and then the children curled up on a sofa and went to sleep. To think that the Land of Stupids would be there tomorrow! How very, very exciting!

Next morning Moonface woke them up. 'Hurry,' he said, 'I've got your breakfast waiting for you. The Land of Stupids is at the top of the tree – I've just been to look – it must have come in the night.'

They ate their breakfast quickly, and then followed Moonface out of his strange little house. The topmost bough of the tree reached up through a hole in the clouds.

'You go up there,' said Moonface, 'and then you come to a little yellow ladder. Climb it and you will find yourself in the Land of Stupids. Goodbye and good luck!'

'Goodbye, my dears,' said their father and gave them each a hug. 'I wish I could come with you, but somebody must look after your mother and the sheep. Goodbye!'

Up the bough climbed the two children and came to the yellow ladder. Up that they went – and suddenly their heads popped out through the cloud – and my goodness me, they found themselves in a sunny green field at the top of the tree. How very strange!

They stood there, gazing all round. In the distance was what looked like a village.

'That must be where the Stupids live!' said

Peter. 'Well, this is the first stage of our journey. We'll go and ask the way to Giantland, and from there we may be able to get to the Land of Storytellers. We're doing well!'

Off they went, and in ten minutes' time they came to the village. But dear me, *what* a village!'

CHAPTER THREE

In the Land of Stupids

The village was full of strangely-built houses. All of them were crooked and many of them seemed about to tumble down. Some had chimneys at the side instead of at the top. A great many had doors near the roof, which had to be reached by ladders.

'What stupid-looking houses!' said Peter. 'Did you ever see anything like them, Mary?'

'I never did!' said the little girl, staring round in astonishment. 'Look at *that* house, Peter! It hasn't any doors at all – only windows!'

'And that house opposite has only doors and no windows at all!' said Peter, beginning to laugh.

It certainly was a strange place – and the people were just as strange! The children soon met some of the Stupids. They were round, fat people, with great big heads and large, staring blue eyes.

'They look like grown-up babies!' said Mary, with a giggle.

They were dressed strangely. Their clothes were all right, but they didn't seem to know how to put them on. Nearly all of them had their coats on back to front, and their buttons were buttoned wrongly. One Stupid went by with a shoe on one foot and a boot on the other.

The children stared at him and could hardly wait to laugh until he had gone by.

'We've got to get to Giantland from here,' said Peter. 'Don't let's spend much time in this silly village, Mary. Let's ask how to get to Giantland, and go on.'

So they stopped the next Stupid and spoke to him. He was a funny-looking creature with a sailor hat on, but as he had it on side-to-front, the ribbon dangled over his nose and made him blink all the time.

'Good morning,' said Peter politely. 'Please could you tell us the way to Giantland?'

The Stupid stared at him and blinked quickly. He made no answer at all.

'Perhaps he's deaf,' said Mary. So she asked the question, this time in a very loud voice.

'PLEASE COULD YOU TELL US THE WAY TO GIANTLAND?'

'It's a long way, but you can get there if you start,' said the Stupid suddenly, as if it was a great effort to answer.

Peter thought that was a silly sort of answer.

'Yes, but which is the way?' he asked.

'Well, there's only one way and that's the right way,' said the Stupid, grinning.

'Of course!' said Peter impatiently. 'But which is the *right* way?'

The Stupid stared at him for a long time, blew the ribbon away from his nose and then scratched his head.

'Ah!' he said at last, very gravely. 'Ah!'

'Ah what?' said the children together, puzzled.

'Oh, just ah!' said the Stupid, and he grinned as if he had said something really very clever.

Peter pulled Mary away, scowling. 'Silly creature!' he grumbled. 'What does he mean with his stupid "Ahs!"? Can't he tell us the way without such a lot of blinking and talking?'

'He certainly was a Stupid!' said Mary, beginning to laugh, as she turned and saw the Stupid watching them, his ribbon dangling over his nose. 'We'll ask someone else. They can't all be as silly as that!'

They walked on down the twisted street. They came to a very crooked little house with two chimneys built in the side, very near the ground. Smoke was pouring out of them and streamed towards a clothes' line on which a small Stupid was putting clothes.

'Just look at that!' said Mary, stopping. 'Did you ever see anything sillier than someone putting out clean clothes where dirty smoke can spoil them!'

They stood and watched the small Stupid. She had a basket full of clean clothes, and these she hung higgledy-piggledy over the line, anyhow. A wind came and blew two of the clothes down to the grass. The Stupid picked them up, shook them and flung them over the line again.

'Why don't you *peg* them on?' called Mary, quite annoyed to see such silliness. She had often hung out the washing for her mother and knew just how it should be done.

'Why should I peg them on?' asked the little Stupid, staring at the children with round blue eyes. 'That would only make more work for me!'

'No, it wouldn't!' said Mary. 'You make far more work for yourself if you *don't* peg them on, because you have to keep picking them up when the wind blows them off – and besides, they will soon get dirty if they keep falling on the ground.'

'Oh, how clever of you!' said the Stupid, in delight. She ran indoors and brought out a box of brand-new pegs that had evidently never been used. She had no idea what to do with them, so Mary pushed open the crooked little gate and went into the garden. In a few minutes she had neatly and tightly pegged up all the

27

clothes in a row, and then no matter how the wind blew, they could not fall.

The little Stupid watched her in admiration.

'Thank you,' she said. 'Thank you very much indeed. They won't fall down now. I never thought of that before. I suppose you couldn't tell me why my clothes always seem so dirty when I come to take them in? No matter how I wash them they always seem full of smuts when I take them indoors to iron.'

'Well, *I* can tell you the reason for that!' said Peter. He pointed to the chimneys that were puffing out black smoke on to the clothes. 'Just look where you've got your clothes' line – right beside those chimneys! The smoke puffs over them all the morning and fills them with smuts. I never saw such a silly place to put a clothes' line!'

The Stupid stared at him open-mouthed.

'You clever boy!' she said. 'You must come with me to the Head-Stupid. He will be so pleased to meet clever people like you.'

'Shall we go and see him?' Peter said to Mary. 'He would know the way to Giantland if anyone would.'

'Yes – let's go,' said Mary. So they let the little Stupid lead them down the street to a bigger house at the end. It was a little more sensibly built than the others, but seemed to have far too many doors. The little Stupid knocked on the biggest door and a voice called 'Come in!'

They opened the door and went in. Inside there was a big room with a large fire-place at one end. Over it a large Stupid was sitting, muffled up in coats and scarves.

'Are you cold?' cried Mary in surprise. 'It's such a lovely day outside!'

The house was full of draughts. The fire smoked badly and the children's eyes were soon smarting. The big Stupid looked at them solemnly.

'Of course I'm cold,' he said, in a grumbling sort of voice. 'So would you be if you lived in a house as draughty as this one! And this wretched fire! No matter what I do to it, it always smokes!'

'Well, why do you have so many doors?' asked Peter, looking round. He counted six doors leading into the one room. How ridiculous! 'No wonder you are always in a draught, and no wonder that your fire smokes, with six doors all round you! And badly fitting doors too!'

'Would that be the reason?' asked the big

Stupid in surprise. 'Dear me, I never thought of that! You must be very, very clever.'

'No, I'm not,' said Peter. 'I'm just an ordinary little boy, but I hope I've got some common sense. If you would have some of these doors taken away and the doorways built up, you would soon find that your room would be as warm as toast and your fire would stop smoking!'

'But it would be better still if you came out-of-doors on this lovely day and got warm in the sunshine!' said Mary.

The big Stupid looked at them with his large blue eyes and seemed to be thinking hard. Then he smiled and nodded. 'You are clever children,' he said. 'I would like your help in some difficulties that are puzzling me.'

'Well, *we* would like your help too,' said Peter. 'Do you know the way to Giantland?'

'Yes,' said the Stupid. 'Yes, I do. I have never been there, but I know the way.'

'How do we get there then?' asked Peter.

'If you'll help me, I'll help you,' said the Stupid, blinking his big staring eyes at them.

'All right. What do you want us to help you with?' asked Peter impatiently. He was getting rather tired of the Stupids.

'I am Head-Stupid and once a day my people come to me with complaints and grumbles,' said the Stupid. 'Perhaps you could tell them what to do?'

'Oh, yes, they could!' said the small Stupid, suddenly and eagerly. She had been standing in a corner, listening, and now she came forward. 'These clever children taught me how to stop the wind from blowing my washing away, and told me why it gets so smutty each week. They could help us a lot, Master!'

'Good,' said the Head-Stupid. 'Ring the bell, please, and tell the people to come round with their grumbles.

The small Stupid ran outside and the children heard her ringing a bell. The Head-Stupid got up and went outside. He sat down on a mat there and beckoned to the children to sit beside him.

Presently up the crooked streets came a crowd of the Stupids. They sat down in a ring round the Head and looked at him with their staring blue eyes. Then one got up and bowed.

'Master, my feet hurt me. What can I do? Shall I have to buy crutches?'

Peter and Mary looked at his feet and began to giggle. The silly creature had got his boots on the wrong feet! No wonder they hurt him!

'Take your boots off and put each one on the other foot!' called Peter. 'Then you will be able to walk comfortably!'

The Stupid unlaced his boots and did as he was told. Then he stood up and walked about. A smile spread over his broad face.

'My feet are healed!' he said. 'I can walk in comfort!'

'Well, don't put your boots on the wrong feet

again, stupid!' said Peter. 'Fancy not knowing your right foot from your left!'

'Master, I cannot see with my glasses,' said a fat little woman, whose shawl was round her waist instead of over her shoulders. She held out her glasses to the Head-Stupid. He gave them to Peter. He could see nothing wrong with them. He put them on and found that they magnified things very much. They were for someone very short-sighted.

He looked at the fat little Stupid. Her eyes looked back quite clearly. Surely she was not short-sighted!

'They are my grandfather's glasses,' she said to Peter. 'I like to wear them in memory of him, but my eyes go wrong when I do.'

Mary began to laugh. Fancy wearing glasses that belonged to someone else and expecting them to suit your own eyes!

'If you take the glass part out and look through the rims you will find that you can see perfectly!' she said, for she was quite sure, and so was Peter, that there was nothing wrong with the Stupid's eyes. The Head-Stupid at once took the glasses from Peter, smashed the glass part, took the splinters from the frame and gave the spectacles back to the woman.

She put them on and gave a cry of delight.

'I can see through my glasses now!' she cried joyfully, blinking through the glassless spectacles. 'My eyes are all right!'

Peter and Mary couldn't help laughing. Why wear the spectacles at all if she could see through them without any glass? But that never once came into the head of the fat little woman!

Then, to Peter's surprise, all the Stupids who were wearing glasses solemnly took them off, broke the glass and put on their spectacles once more – without any glass in them.

'Much better, much better!' they said gravely nodding to one another. The children stared in surprise. Were there ever such stupid people! They thought that *one* person's mistake must be everyone's!

'Please, Master, I can't reach my coat pockets no matter how I try!' said another Stupid, coming forward. The children looked at him. He was very plump, and as he had put on his coat back to front – and, of course, buttoned it all wrong – he found it was impossible to reach round to his pockets, which were now at the back instead of at the front.

'Take off your coat, put it on the other way, and you'll find you can reach your pockets,' said Peter at once.

The Stupid did so – and when he found that

he could then put his hands into all his pockets he was overjoyed. He pulled out all sorts of things and examined them carefully, as if he hadn't seen them for months – which, Peter thought, was quite likely, as it would never occur to him to look through the pockets when he had the coat off!

'Clever, very clever!' cried everyone admiringly.

One after another the Stupids asked their silly questions, which the children found easy to answer. When everyone had finished, Peter turned to the Head-Stupid.

'Now we've helped you as we said we would,' he said. 'Will you tell us the way to Giantland?'

'Well, it's dinner-time now,' said the big Stupid. 'Let's have something to eat.'

They went inside the smoky house and two little Stupids set a table. They set it very badly, the children thought, for they put the knives on the left-hand side and the forks on the right.

'Just as if we were all left-handed!' Mary whispered to Peter. The meal was served the wrong way round, too. The pudding came first, and then the meat and vegetables!

'Now it's time for a nap,' said the Head-Stupid, and he straightway lay down on his unmade bed and began to snore.

The children stared at him crossly. What a lot of time they were wasting! Why couldn't he have told them the way to Giantland before he went to sleep.

'Let's wake him up,' said Peter. So they dug him in the ribs and clapped him on the shoulder. But he simply turned over on his other side and snored even more loudly. Then Mary took a sponge that was, of all funny places, lying in the coal scuttle, filled it with water and squeezed it over the Stupid's face. Still he didn't wake!

'It's no good,' said Peter in disgust. 'I believe he's pretending to be asleep just so that he shan't tell us our way.'

The children did not get away from the Land of Stupids that day, for the Head-Stupid slept until six o'clock and then he wanted his supper. He kept putting the children off until they both became angry.

'You are very mean!' burst out Peter suddenly. 'We've kept our part of the bargain. Why don't you keep yours? If you *don't* know the way to Giantland why don't you say so?'

'But I *do* know it!' said the Head-Stupid annoyingly. 'And don't you speak to me like that, or I'll have you locked up!'

'Whatever for!' cried Mary indignantly. 'Can't we tell you if we think you're not playing fair? You great silly Stupid, I don't believe you know what it is to keep a promise!'

The Stupid clapped his hands five times and four more Stupids came in at once. They wore what was supposed to be policemen's uniform, but somehow it had got all wrong. Their helmets were on sideways and were so big that the children could only see the mouths of the Stupids. Their coats, as usual, were back to front, and their trousers far too short. Instead of heavy boots they wore fancy bedroom slippers with blue rosettes on, and this made Mary laugh loudly.

'Lock them up for the night,' said the Head-Stupid – and to the children's dismay they were marched off to a little round house that was a sort of police cell, for it had bars on its only window, and a great bolt on its one door.

'Well, they seem to know how to build a prison all right,' said Peter gloomily, looking through the bars. 'It's too bad, Mary. We shall never get away!'

'I expect they don't want us to go,' said Mary. 'We are much too useful to them! I'm sure they'd like to keep us here to answer all their silly questions and to put everything right for them, just as long as ever they could!'

Peter stared at Mary, and then he answered her in excitement.

'Mary, I do believe you're right! That's why they won't tell us what we want to know! They don't want us to go! We're too useful! They'll try to keep us here as long as they can!'

'Oh dear!' said Mary in dismay. 'How ever can we get away?'

'We can't, if they lock us up like this,' said Peter, trying to see if he could force out the bars on the window. 'They may be stupid in most things — but they are clever enough to know how to keep what they want!'

The children sat frowning together in the little cell. There was a mattress there and one chair. That was all. There was no way of escaping. Outside they could hear the tramp of their four guards.

Suddenly Peter smiled to himself. Mary saw him. 'What are you smiling for?' she asked.

'I've thought of a way to beat the Stupids, Mary!' said Peter. 'Listen!' He dropped his voice to a whisper, so that if any of the guards were listening they could not hear. 'Tomorrow we will be even stupider than the Stupids! We won't be able to answer their questions, or, if we do, we'll answer them so stupidly that the silly creatures will think we're no use to them, and let us go. See?'

'Oh, yes!' said Mary at once. 'That's a very good idea. If they think we're not so clever after all they won't bother to keep us! That's what we'll do, Peter — we'll be as stupid as they are!'

They fell asleep soon after that and did not wake until the morning. The four guards unbolted the door and marched them out. They had breakfast with the Head-Stupid, who asked them most politely how they had slept.

'How did I sleep? Well, I slept with my eyes closed, I think,' said Peter solemnly, with a very stupid expression on his face, which made Mary giggle. The Head-Stupid said nothing more. He gave Peter a scornful look and went on with his breakfast. It was just as funny a breakfast as the dinner had been. It began with marmalade and toast and went on to bacon and eggs, finishing up with porridge!

'I want you to come and help me with my people's complaints again,' said the Head-Stupid, when they had all finished.

'Certainly,' said Peter, taking the Head-Stupid's hat and putting it on back to front. He looked so silly that Mary couldn't help giggling. She wished she could think of something silly to do too, such as taking off her socks and wearing them on her hands, but it was too much trouble! The Head-Stupid probably wouldn't notice, anyway!

When the bell rang the Stupids all came round again with their complaints and their grumbles. But this time the children were most unhelpful!

'My clock won't go!' said one Stupid, holding up a big clock. Peter felt certain that the Stupid had forgotten to wind it up, but he didn't say so. He took the clock gravely, shook it, turned it upside down and then handed it back.

'No, it won't go,' he said, and would say no more. The Head-Stupid frowned at him, but Peter pretended not to notice.

'I can't do up this coat I've just made,' complained another Stupid. She held up her coat and Mary saw that she had made all the button holes and stitched all the buttons on the same side of the coat – so of course she couldn't do it up! Mary took the coat and pretended to try to button it. Then she shook her head and handed it back to the anxious Stupid.

'It won't do up,' said Mary, and that was all *she* would say!

They would tell the Stupids nothing that morning and the Head-Stupid became more and more impatient. At last he lost his temper.

'I thought you were clever!' he stormed. 'I thought you knew more than we did! You are even sillier than the silliest Stupid in the village. I don't know how you managed to deceive me yesterday!'

'We told you we weren't clever,' said Peter. 'We are just an ordinary boy and girl.'

'Well you're no use to *us*!' said the Head-Stupid. 'You'd better go!'

'That's just what we want to do!' said Peter. 'Which is the way to Giantland?'

'I shan't tell you!' said the Head-Stupid meanly. 'Find out for yourself.'

Peter and Mary stared at him in disgust. What a mean horrid person he was! 'Come on, Mary,' said Peter, taking her hand. 'We'll leave this foolish place. Its people are even too stupid to have any manners!'

He put his hat on straight and the two children walked away from the village. They had no idea which way to go, but they thought they might perhaps meet someone who could tell them. Soon they had left the crooked houses behind and were on a high road. There was no one in sight at all.

They walked on in the hot sun and presently they saw that the road forked into three ways. Which one ought they to take?

'There's a signpost, Peter!' cried Mary suddenly, pointing to a three-fingered post standing not far off. 'It's got names on it. It's sure to say which way Giantland is!'

They ran to it. The first arm, pointing to the right, said 'This way to Giantland'.

'Good!' said Peter. 'We'll go that way.' Then he stopped and stared at the next arm, pointing to the left. It said 'Take this road to Giantland'.

'That's strange,' said Mary, puzzled. 'They can't *both* go to the same place, surely!'

The third arm said 'To Giantland, this way'.

'Why, all the roads seem to lead to Giantland, Mary,' said Peter, more puzzled than ever.

'Well, maybe Giantland is so big that it stretches in all directions,' said Mary wisely. 'Let's take the middle road. We're almost sure to be right then. If Giantland lies to the right *and* the left, there must be some in the middle too!'

'You're quite right!' said Peter. So they took the middle road, wondering very much what the land of Giants would be like.

CHAPTER FOUR

Among the Giants

The two children walked on for some time, and then coming behind them, they heard a noise like rolling thunder. They turned round in surprise – and saw a curious sight. The noise was made by the wheels of a most enormous cart, drawn by a horse as big as an elephant!

'Goodness!' cried Peter, pulling Mary to one side. 'Look at that! We must certainly be on the road to Giantland because there is a giant horse and cart.'

'And a giant driving them!' said Mary, peeping out from the bush in which she was hiding. The giant was humming a song as he passed by, and the sound was like the throbbing of an aeroplane. The children gazed at him in awe, for he was simply enormous. His eyes were as big as saucers, and his thick hair hung round his great head like ropes.

'I hope the giants don't see us as we go through their land,' said Peter, rather uneasily, when the horse and cart had thundered past. 'It wouldn't do to be caught by them, Mary. The best thing we can do is to keep to the side of the road among the bushes and hide whenever we see anyone coming. When we get to a village or a town we had better hide until night and then creep through it when it is dark.'

'That's a good idea,' said Mary. 'If the giants see us they will think we are dwarfs, we shall seem so tiny to them! We had far better keep out of their way. We shall come to another signpost sooner or later, and that will tell us the way to the Land of Storytellers – and then, hurrah! We'll soon find Fenella and get her home again!'

They felt happy as they walked on their way once more. It didn't seem very difficult to get through Giantland and then on to the place where Fenella was. They skipped along, until Peter noticed something strange.

'Look, Mary!' he said suddenly, stopping and pointing to the grass and the bushes they were passing. 'Do you notice how the grass seems to be getting taller and taller? And look at the trees! They are stretching up to the sky and their trunks are nearly as thick as the trunk of that big Faraway Tree we climbed in the Enchanted Wood.'

Sure enough it was true. The grasses were soon taller than the children, and the bushes seemed like young woods!

'It's *really* Giantland now!' said Mary. We shall find it very easy to hide, Peter. No giant will see us in this tall grass!'

They kept among the grass as much as they could. But not only the grass was giant-like; the insects were too! A large brown thing, with ugly-looking pincers at its tail-end, suddenly hurried by, nearly knocking Mary over.

'What was that?' she said to Peter, going quite pale. 'Was it a sort of dragon?'

'No,' said Peter, laughing. 'It was only a giant earwig! And look, whatever's that?'

It was a monstrous ladybird, her spotted back gleaming like a mirror, it was so bright. As she drew near to the children she stopped in alarm. She unfolded some gauzy wings from underneath her spotted back, spread them and flew away with a little buzzing noise.

'There she goes!' said Peter. 'A ladybird almost as big as a puppy!'

They went on, Peter keeping a sharp lookout for other creatures. They saw a great spider, its eight legs covered with thick hairs, looking at them from eight eyes set on its forehead. It did look strange and ugly. Peter was half-afraid it might think they were insects to be eaten, and he hurried Mary on as quickly as he could. They had to look out for webs, too, for Peter thought it would be a difficult thing to get out of a sticky web once they had blundered into it.

Soon they heard a crashing noise, and the children crouched down behind a tall butter-cup, whose golden head waved high above them. An animal as big as a donkey came bounding through the grass. It was an enor-mous rabbit, its big ears twitching as it stopped just by the children listening.

After some while the children came to a village. The houses all seemed as big as castles, so that to them the village seemed a vast town. Great carts thundered by, and enormous dogs sniffed about. Peter was afraid a dog might smell them out, and he looked round for a hiding-place.

He saw a hole not far off and took Mary to it. It was as big as a small tunnel. They squeezed down it and not far down found a kind of room hollowed out, lined with moss and leaves. It was quite cosy, but smelt rather musty.

'Does it belong to anyone, do you think?' said Mary.

'I shouldn't think so,' said Peter.

But it did! For suddenly there came a smooth, gliding sound and down the hole came a large round worm, soft and slimy! It had no eyes and could not see that there was anyone in its hole. It coiled itself round the children, and, when they struggled and shouted, let go in alarm. It shot up the hole again and disappeared.

'What a shock it got, poor thing!' said Mary.

'What a shock *we* got, too!' said Peter. 'We had better go, Mary. The worm might have gone to get his friends to turn us out, and as they are as big as pythons it wouldn't be very pleasant. Come on!'

So out of the hole they crept, and went to look for another hiding place. Soon something strange happened. Great blobs of water bigger than dinner plates fell round them! One hit Peter on the head and knocked him over.

'Whatever is it!' he cried, shaking the water from him.

'It's raining!' said Mary. 'Giant rain! How strange! Come under this big thistle, Peter, till it stops.'

The thistle was a tall, prickly plant with its spines as long as spears. The children had to be careful not to get pricked or cut. They crouched under the broad thistle leaves and heard the raindrops falling around them thickly, and soon, to the children's great dismay, a little stream of water appeared behind the thistle.

'Oh my, I hope a puddle isn't going to come just here!' groaned Peter. The water spread around them. It was most annoying. If only they had chosen another plant to shelter under they could have climbed up its stem and sat on a leaf. But the thistle was set with such long sharp prickles that it was impossible to climb.

Just as the puddle was closing round the

children's feet a large white thing came sailing by. Peter and Mary stared at it.

'It's an enormous paper boat!' cried Mary, in surprise. 'Some giant boy or girl must have made it and set it sailing in the rain puddles. It's big enough for us to get into, Peter. Shall we stop it and climb inside?'

'Yes,' said Peter. 'The rain is stopping now, so we shan't get very wet if we sail off in the boat. Come on!'

He caught hold of the paper side of the boat and held it still whilst Mary stepped into it. Then Peter got in too. The boat swung round the prickly thistle and then rushed off down the stream of water, which was now as large as a river. The children clung to the paper middle of the boat. Along they went, now rushing to one side and now to another.

'Peter! I believe this boat is taking us to the village!' said Mary, in alarm.

'We'd better get out then,' said Peter. But by now the boat was going along far too fast. Sometimes it spun round and round and made the children giddy. They wished they had never climbed into it!

Suddenly the stream of water ran under a sort of bridge and came out into the gutter of a roadway! Peter and Mary stared in horror. They

were in the village where the giants lived, just
the place they had been trying to keep away
from whilst it was daylight! Now here they
were, tearing along the gutter in a paper boat for
all the giants to see! It was dreadful!

One or two giants were walking down the
wide street, holding great umbrellas up to keep
off the few drops of rain still falling. Nobody
noticed the children at first – and then a little
giant-girl saw them and shouted in excitement.

'Look! Look! Two little dolls in a boat!'

The giant-mother looked. The giant-girl ran
to the gutter and picked up the boat, with Peter

51

and Mary still in it. She picked them up so carelessly that Mary nearly fell out.

'Be careful!' yelled Peter, clutching hold of Mary's arm and just saving her in time. 'Be careful, giant-girl! You'll make us fall!'

The girl was so astonished to hear Peter's voice that she very nearly dropped the boat.

'Mother! They are not dolls, they are real!' she cried, in surprise.

'Well I never!' boomed the mother-giant, in amazement. 'Two little mannikins! Wherever could they have come from? We'll take them home, Grizel.'

'Put them in your market-bag, Mother,' said Grizel, the giant-girl. So into the mother's net-bag went Peter and Mary, among potatoes, cakes and a large cabbage whose thick leaves felt like leather.

They were carried in the bag for a long way. Peter found himself squashed against a delicious chocolate cake. As he was very hungry he thought he might as well make a meal whilst he had the chance. So he whispered to Mary, who was sitting in a cabbage leaf, and the two children took big handfuls of the cake and ate it.

At last they were taken into a great house and the giant-girl emptied them out of the bag.

'They are really alive,' said the mother-giant.

'Take them up to your nursery, Grizel. You will like them better than your dolls.'

So up to the nursery went Grizel, carrying Mary and Peter, one in each hand. She held them rather tightly so that they could hardly breathe, but at least they were not afraid of falling.

Grizel shut the door and set the children on the floor. There were enormous toys all round, all of them bigger than the children. In the corner stood a doll's house, not quite as big as a small, ordinary house would be to us. A large rocking-horse towered above the children and balls as high as an ordinary room were here and there. It was all rather frightening.

'Now I'm going to have a lovely game with you!' said Grizel, in delight. 'I'm going to play at being the old woman who lived in the shoe, and you shall be my children. I shall cook you some broth without any bread, and then I shall whip you soundly and put you to bed!'

Peter and Mary listed in horror. Good gracious, a smack from Grizel's huge hand would knock them flat. What an unpleasant child she must be!

Grizel got out a cooking-stove, a toy one to her, but as big as a real one to the children. She poured some water into a saucepan, scraped into it a bit of carrot, a speck of onion and a morsel of turnip, and then set them on the stove to cook.

'Goodness! Is that the broth!' said Peter to Mary. 'I jolly well won't eat it!'

Grizel took two small chairs out of her doll's house and sat the children down firmly on them. Peter was cross and jumped up again. *He* wasn't going to be sat down and stood up like a doll!

'Oh, naughty, naughty!' said Grizel. She tapped him with her finger and Peter shouted in pain, for the big girl's finger was as large as a log of wood, and bruised his shoulder dreadfully. He sat down again at once. It was no use offending a giant, even if she was only a small one!

Grizel took out a doll's table and set it before the children. She laid out small knives and forks and two dishes. By this time the broth was cooking, so she ladled some out of the saucepan into their dishes. It was steaming hot.

'There you are, children,' she said. 'Eat up your broth.'

Neither Peter nor Mary took up their spoons, for they could see the broth was too hot. Grizel picked up a spoon, filled it with the hot broth and tried to make Mary drink it. It burnt

Mary's mouth and she shouted in pain. Up jumped Peter in a rage and knocked over the dish of broth. It fell on to the giant-girl's foot and scalded her. She danced round, crying.

'Well, you shouldn't make Mary drink something that's too hot!' shouted Peter. 'It serves you right!'

But that was a silly thing to say to hot-tempered Grizel. She picked Peter up, slapped him hard, so that all the breath was forced out of him, and then took him to the doll's house. She opened the front of it, and put him into a small bed there.

'You *deserve* to be smacked soundly and put to bed!' scolded the giant-girl. She went back to Mary, slapped her too, and put her into another bed, just by Peter. Then she slammed shut the big front of the doll's house and left them.

Mary was crying. Peter, feeling all his bones to make sure that the rough giant-girl hadn't broken any, sat up in his bed.

'Are you hurt, Mary?' he called anxiously.

'No, only bruised where that great rough girl slapped me,' wept Mary. 'Oh, Peter, isn't this a horrible adventure? Oh, whatever are we going to do?'

Peter got out of bed and went to the window of the doll's house. He looked out.

'I don't know,' he said gloomily. 'The nursery door is shut and we shall never be able to climb up as high as the window.'

Just then the nursery door was flung open and in danced Grizel, her steps as loud as thunder. She went to the doll's house and peeped in at the window.

'Mother's letting me have a party this afternoon to show you off!' she called. 'All my friends are coming and we'll play lovely games

with you! You'll be like real, live dolls! I'll come
and get you ready in an hour's time. Some of my
doll's best clothes will fit you nicely.'

She danced out again, banging the door
behind her. She really was a very noisy person
indeed. Peter had fled back to bed as soon as he
had heard her coming. He didn't want to be
slapped again!

'Oh, Mary, did you hear what she said?' he
groaned. 'A party to show us off! That means
we'll be picked up and handled and squeezed
and squashed by lots more giant children like
Grizel. What in the world can we do?'

'Well, Peter, can't we hide somewhere?' said
Mary, getting out of bed. 'Grizel won't be
coming back for an hour. That's a long time.
Surely we can find somewhere in this big
nursery where we can hide safely till it's
night.'

'Yes, we'll hide!' said Peter. He jumped out
of the doll's bed once more and he and Mary
went down the little doll's house stairs together.
They opened the front door and looked out.
Where would be the best place to hide?

'There's a space under the toy cupboard.
Shall we hide there?' said Mary. But Peter
shook his head.

'No,' he said. 'They'd be sure to look there.

We must hide in some place where they'll never dream of looking.'

They began to hunt round. Should they hide in the box of bricks? No, that was much too dangerous. They might be tipped out with the bricks. What about in the coal-scuttle? No, it was very dirty, and besides, they might be put on the fire with the coal.

'Shall we get into one of the trucks belonging to the toy train?' said Peter. 'It's quite big enough to take us. We should be safe there.'

'*I* don't think we should,' said Mary. 'Grizel would look there, I'm sure. What about squeezing under the carpet, Peter?'

'That's silly,' said Peter, at once. 'We might be trodden on.'

The children looked round in despair. Wherever *could* they hide? They had already spent quite half-an-hour hunting here and there. And then a sound startled them dreadfully. It was a very loud voice indeed, crying 'Cuckoo! Cuckoo! Cuckoo!'

Mary clutched hold of Peter and looked round for the voice. Did it belong to another giant?

Then Peter pointed upwards and began to laugh.

'Look! It's a cuckoo clock!' he said. 'It's like

the one we've got at home. The cuckoo comes out of that little door at the top to call the hour.'

Mary stared up at it – and then a great idea came to her.

'Peter! Why shouldn't we hide in the little room where the cuckoo lives, at the top of the clock? No one would ever find us there!'

Peter shouted with delight.

'Good for you, Mary! The best idea you've ever thought of! Look, the clock has long winding-up chains reaching right to the floor, just as our clock at home has. We can easily climb up by putting our feet into the links of the chain.'

They ran to the chains that hung from the giant cuckoo clock. They could easily put their feet into the links. Up they went, the chains swaying as they climbed. It was a long climb, and the children's arms ached long before they reached the clock.

The clock was carved with leaves and birds. Peter and Mary swung themselves up on to a wooden leaf and climbed round the clock-face until they reached the little door at the top of the clock, behind which the cuckoo lived. Peter tried to open the door, but he couldn't.

'We'll wait until the cuckoo comes out next time and then slip in,' said Peter.

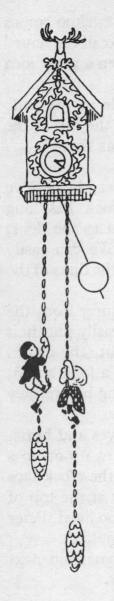

'But the next time it cuckoos it will be half-past three, and by that time Grizel will be here looking for us,' whispered Mary.

'Oh, goodness, I forgot that!' said Peter in dismay. He tugged at the door – but it would *not* open!

'We must crouch behind a leaf and hope that Grizel won't think of looking up here,' he said at last. So he and Mary squeezed themselves behind a carved leaf and waited. It was not very long before the nursery door flew open once more and in rushed the giant-girl. She went to the doll's house and opened the front of it.

'Come along, you little live dolls!' she called. 'It's time you were dressed for my party!'

Then she saw that they were not there! She gave a cry of rage and tumbled all the furniture of the little house out on to the floor, looking for them.

Then she jumped to her feet and shouted 'Mother! Mother! Those dolls have gone! Come and help me look for them! They must be hiding!'

Into the room came the giant-mother, dressed in her best. She and Grizel began to hunt round for the children. Peter and Mary trembled to see them.

'Just wait till I find them!' grumbled Grizel angrily. 'I'll give them such a smacking!'

'Is the cuckoo going to call the half-hour soon?' whispered Mary to Peter. 'We mustn't miss it, Peter.'

'We shall hear a whirring noise when it is going to come out and cuckoo,' whispered back Peter. 'Cheer up, Mary.'

They waited anxiously for the whirring noise. They were dreadfully afraid that the giants would look up and see them very soon. At last they heard the whirring noise inside the clock that meant that the cuckoo was getting ready to come out. Peter reached over and took Mary's hand.

Whizz! The little wooden door flew open, and out came the cuckoo, flapping small painted wings.

'Cuckoo!' the children heard.

At once Mary and Peter slipped in at the open door. The cuckoo jerked back and the door slammed shut. They were in the little room belonging to the cuckoo in the clock!

CHAPTER FIVE

Inside the
Cuckoo Clock

It was very dark there at first. Outside, the children could hear Grizel and her mother getting crosser and crosser.

'They're not under the cupboard!'

'They're not in the brick box!'

'They're not in any of the train trucks!'

'Where *can* they be? Bother them! It's too bad! I can hear our guests arriving downstairs, and now there are no wonderful live dolls to show them!'

'Have they climbed up behind any of the pictures?'

Then the children heard all the pictures being slightly turned, and they were glad to think that they had slipped inside the cuckoo-clock before the giants had thought of looking upwards. They might easily have been seen on the clock, whilst they were waiting for the cuckoo.

Gradually they began to be able to see what the inside of the cuckoo's little room was like – and then, what an enormous surprise they got!

It was a proper little room. There was a round table in the middle with a blue check cloth on it. There were chairs about and a shining cupboard in one corner. There was a tiny fire at the back of the room with a small kettle boiling away merrily – and sitting by it in a rocking chair was – the cuckoo!

At first the children thought the cuckoo was an old woman, sitting there knitting – but no, it was most certainly the cuckoo! She had a red shawl thrown over her shoulders, and she had slipped her feet into a pair of old slippers. There she sat, with spectacles on her nose, knitting away for dear life!

The children stared and stared. They didn't know what to say or do. This was the most surprising thing they had ever seen!

Presently the cuckoo lifted her head and looked at them twinklingly over her spectacles.

'Have you quite finished looking at me?' she asked, in a soft, cuckooing sort of voice. 'Am I such a surprise? Well, I can assure you that you are every bit as much of a surprise to *me*!' This is the first time I've ever had any visitors since I came here. It is most exciting.'

'We didn't know – we really didn't know you were properly alive and lived in a little room like this,' said Mary, finding her voice at last. 'We just thought we'd come and hide in the clock.'

'And a very good idea too,' said the cuckoo, knitting away steadily. 'Nobody would think of looking for you here. You are quite safe. I heard those giants looking for you down there. I'm glad Grizel didn't find you. She's a careless, spiteful creature. She often forgets to wind up this clock and then I can't go out of my door for days.'

'Do you mind us hiding here?' asked Peter.

'Not a bit,' said the cuckoo. 'I tell you I'm delighted to have someone to talk to. I do get so lonely up here in my little room. What about a bite of tea, now? Are you hungry?'

'Very,' said Peter, at once. 'Our dinner was only some chocolate cake in the giant's marketing-bag.'

'Can I help you?' asked Mary politely.

'Well that would be most kind of you,' said the cuckoo. 'My legs are rather bad today and I'd be glad to have someone waiting on me for a change. All the tea-things are in that cupboard over there. You can make the tea, and the boy can make us some toast. There are some sausages in the cupboard. We'll fry those too.'

'Will the giants hear us talking up here?' asked Mary anxiously.

'Bless you, no!' said the cuckoo comfortably. 'They don't know anything about my snug little room here. I heard it was to let years ago and came here, and here I've been ever since, with never a soul to peep in at me or say how do you do! So long as I cuckoo every half-hour and every hour that's all the giants care about!'

Soon the children were busy over the tea. Mary set the little table neatly, and Peter made a pile of toast. Then, whilst he fried the

sausages – and dear me, *how* good they smelt
– the little girl made the tea.

'It's all ready, Mistress Cuckoo!' she said.

The cuckoo brought her rocking-chair to the
table and began to pour out the tea. Then she
served the sausages, and the children ate them
hungrily.

'This is a great treat for me,' said the kindly
cuckoo, beaming at the children down her long
beak. 'I do enjoy company and it's years since
I had any. Now where did I put my best
strawberry jam and those shortbread biscuits
I've been saving up?' She got up and went to the
cupboard. She found a large jar and a big tin.

Just as she was about to put them on the table the children were most astonished to see her turn herself about and rush swiftly to the door. She pushed it open and went out.

'Where's she gone?' asked Mary, in alarm. 'She isn't going to tell the giants about us, is she?'

'Cuckoo! Cuckoo! Cuckoo! Cuckoo!' called the cuckoo, in her loud, clear voice. Then she came back with a rush, slammed the door and put the jar and the tin on the table. She sank down on her chair and began to laugh.

'Oh my, oh my!' she said. 'Do you know, I almost forgot to cuckoo the hour! As it was I was two minutes late! Fancy that! And I went to the door carrying my tin and my jar of jam, and with my red shawl on! Whatever would the giants have thought if they had seen me? I really don't know! They would have taken the clock down at once and looked inside my room, there's no doubt!'

'Then we've had quite an escape,' said Peter, rather alarmed. 'We won't let you forget to cuckoo at the half-hour, Mistress Cuckoo!'

'No, please don't,' said the cuckoo, putting out some delicious-looking strawberry jam into a flowered china dish. 'I've never forgotten before. It was just the excitement of having visitors that made me forget. Now do have some jam with your buttered toast!'

The children ate an enormous tea. The jam was lovely, and the shortbread biscuits melted away in their mouths. Peter kept looking at his watch as the time went on.

'It's almost the half-hour, Mistress Cuckoo!' he said suddenly. At once the cuckoo got up, threw off her shawl and her slippers and went to open the door. She cuckooed loudly once and came back again.

'The nursery is full of giant children,' she said. 'It's the party going on, I expect. Can you hear the noise?'

The children listened. The cuckoo's room was high up and quiet, but they could quite well hear the loud shouts and heavy footfalls of the children below. They trembled to think that they might have been down there with them, being handled and squeezed.

'Don't look so frightened!' said the cuckoo, now quite comfortable again in her shawl and slippers. 'You're safe here. I wish you'd live with me always, I do like you so much.'

'We'd love to stay with you for a long time,' said Mary, smiling at the kindly cuckoo. 'But we are trying to rescue someone who has been captured by a wicked gnome, and we mustn't stay too long. Peter, you tell Mistress Cuckoo all about it.'

'We'd better clear away and wash up first,' said Peter, looking at the littered table. So the children set to work, much to the delight of the cuckoo, who had never been waited on before. They soon cleared the table and washed up in a little sink that was neatly hidden by a small red curtain. They put away all the things and then went to sit down by the fire. The cuckoo was rocking herself busily, still knitting.

'Now tell me all about yourselves,' she said cosily. 'You can't possibly go tonight, so take your time about it. I am so enjoying having you both!'

Peter told the cuckoo all his story, from the dreadful moment when Fenella disappeared to the time when he and Mary had climbed up the clock-chains. The cuckoo nodded her head and said 'Dear, dear!' now and then.

'Well!' she said, when Peter had finished, 'I do think you are two dear, brave children to set out on such a journey, and I hope you'll find Fenella. I do, indeed!'

'Do you know the best way to get from here to the Land of Storytellers?' asked Peter. 'Is it a very long way?'

'Well,' said the cuckoo, putting down her knitting, 'it *is* rather a long way. You see, Giantland is so big that it stretches for miles and miles and miles. I really don't know how you could walk through it without being seen a hundred times by the giants.'

'Oh, dear!' said Peter, in dismay, 'I don't want to be caught by giants again! Once is quite enough!'

'I should think so!' said the cuckoo.

'I suppose there's no way of *flying* over Giantland is there?' asked Mary. 'That would be so much better than walking all the way through it!'

'No – there's no aeroplane or anything,' said the cuckoo thoughtfully. 'I don't see *how* you could fly over – unless – unless –'

'Unless what?' cried the children excitedly.

'Well – unless *I* took you on my back and flew over Giantland!' said the cuckoo slowly.

The children stared at her.

'But *would* you?' asked Peter eagerly.

'I don't see why I shouldn't,' said the cuckoo, taking off her glasses and looking at the children. 'I used to be able to fly very well indeed. I shall have to practise a bit tonight, when the giants are all in bed. I could take a few turns round the nursery and see if my wings are

71

as strong as they used to be. Oh, I could fly very swiftly and well when I was younger!'

Mary jumped up and hugged the cuckoo till she gasped for breath and begged for mercy.

'You're a perfect dear to help us like this!' said Mary. 'Oh, how lovely it would be if we could miss out the rest of Giantland by flying right over it! I don't like the giants one bit.'

'Well, now, we can't do anything about it just yet,' said the cuckoo, rolling up her knitting and putting it into a black bag. 'What about a game of Snap? It's ages since I had a good game with anyone!'

'Oh let's!' cried the children. So the cuckoo got out a pack of curious snap-cards, all with giant-families on them, and they sat round the table and played until they were tired. Every half-hour the cuckoo had to get up and rush to the door to cuckoo, and once she took her snap-cards with her, she was in such a hurry. How they all laughed when she came back, looking flustered and hot!

'Do you know, I nearly called "Snap!" instead of "Cuckoo!"' she said to the children. 'Whatever would the giants have thought?'

That made the children laugh even more. They had a lovely game until the cuckoo said it was time to stop and have supper. Mary and

Peter put her in her rocking-chair again and said they would manage supper.

'There is a jam-tart in the cupboard, and you'll find some cream in a blue jug!' said the cuckoo, getting out her knitting again. 'Make a jug of hot cocoa, and that will suit us all nicely!'

They had supper all together, joking and laughing. There was gooseberry jam in the tart, and plenty of sugar in the cocoa. It was great fun. After that the children cleared away and washed up. Then Mary yawned.

'Aha, it's bedtime for you!' said the cuckoo.

'Oh, no, do let me see you fly round the nursery!' begged Mary.

'Very well,' said the cuckoo. 'I'll just go and peep out to see if everything is safe.'

She went to her little door and pushed it open. The nursery was dark except for some light that came into it from the landing outside, where a big lamp burned.

'It's quite safe, I think,' said the cuckoo, peering out. She took off her shawl, which was wrapped round her wings and prevented her from spreading them properly. Peter and Mary went to the door and watched.

The cuckoo spread her wings and launched herself into the air. Round and round the nursery she went, flapping her wings. At last she came back quite delighted.

'My wings are even stronger because of the long rest I've had!' she said, pleased. 'I shall be able to carry you both very easily. Just half a minute!'

She turned to the nursery and cuckooed loudly ten times. It was ten o'clock!

'Now,' she said briskly, wrapping herself up in her shawl again and slamming the door. 'Now, it's time for bed! We must all get to sleep quickly, because my plan is that we set out at dawn, when all the giants are still asleep. With luck we should reach the land of Storytellers about eight o'clock, and I can be back in my clock before lunchtime. Perhaps no one will notice I am not cuckooing. Very often the giants are out all the morning shopping.'

The children were happy and very sleepy. Mary could hardly keep her eyes open.

'Where shall we sleep?' asked Peter, looking all round. He could not see a bed anywhere.

The cuckoo went to the wall and pressed a little knob. A panel slid aside and the cuckoo pulled out a neat little bed, complete with blankets and pillows.

'You have to hide things away when your room is as small as mine!' she said. 'Now there's just room for the two of you there. Undress and get in quickly, or you'll fall asleep where you're standing!'

'But where will *you* sleep?' asked Mary.

'In my rocking-chair,' said the cuckoo. 'I often take a nap there. I've got to be out of my door, cuckooing every half-hour, so my nights are never very peaceful. Now hurry up, both of you!'

Soon the children were tucked up in the small, but very soft and comfortable bed. They closed their eyes and fell fast asleep in two minutes! The cuckoo sat down in her rocking chair and took up her knitting. She was very happy. It was such a treat to have two cheerful, friendly visitors. She would remember this day for years and years!

At dawn she awakened the sleeping children. 'Time to be off!' she said. 'I've made some hot coffee for us, and there's some bacon and eggs cooking. They will be ready by the time you are dressed!'

The children smelt the good smell of frying bacon and hot coffee. They dressed quickly and were soon sitting down at the little round table enjoying their breakfast.

'There's not a soul awake in the house!' said the cuckoo, drinking her coffee. 'Not a soul!

We shall be able to fly off without anyone seeing us!

'What's that funny noise?' asked Mary, listening to a strange throbbing noise that rose and fell all the time.

'Oh, that's just the giants snoring,' said the cuckoo. 'They all do that. Now what about some marmalade with your toast, Peter?'

They all made a good breakfast and then the cuckoo gave some apples and chocolate to the children to take with them. She took off her shawl and gave it to Mary.

'I can't fly with it on,' she said. 'But you'd better use it as a rug to cover yourselves when you're on my back. The morning air is chilly. I shall keep my slippers on. I do have such dreadful chilblains if I don't. Now are we ready?' The children took a last look round the dear little room where they had been so kindly treated. Then they climbed on to the cuckoo's broad back and wrapped the red shawl round them. The cuckoo opened the door, told them to hold tight, and spread her wings.

Off they went into the air, circling round the nursery! The window was a little bit open at the top and the cuckoo flapped neatly through the crack and out into the cold morning air. The sun was just rising, and everything was touched with gold.

'Isn't this fun?' shouted Peter to Mary. 'Weren't we lucky to find such a kind friend?'

Mary cuddled herself into the shawl, for the morning was certainly cold. She smiled at Peter, and then looked down at Giantland. It was a strange place in the early sunlight. The houses towered up like enormous castles. The windows seemed endless, and shone brilliantly in the sun. The streets were very wide, and the cats that lay about here and there were as big as donkeys.

On and on flew the cuckoo, flapping her strong wings. For hour after hour she flew, and the children grew a little sleepy again, for they had not had a very long night. Mary yawned. The cuckoo heard her and turned her head.

'Why don't you try to get a nap?' she called in her soft, cuckooing voice. 'You will be quite safe on my back if you tuck your feet well into the fold of my wings.'

So for some while the children slept, their feet tucked into the warm folds of the cuckoo's wings, and their hands clinging to her neck-feathers. The sun rose higher and beat down warmly. Mary suddenly awoke, feeling far too hot.

She sat up and took off the shawl. Then she awoke Peter in excitement.

'Peter! I do believe we are out of Giantland now! Look down! The houses are no longer big.'

They looked down. It was quite true. They had passed right over Giantland and were now in another land. They called to the cuckoo.

'Yes!' she said, 'we are over the Land of Storytellers now. I'm taking you to the market-place as you will no doubt find plenty of people there to ask about the gnome Sly-One. We shall be there in two minutes.'

In a short time the cuckoo flew down to a crowded market-place, where gnomes of all kinds bought and sold, chattering and calling at the tops of their hoarse voices.

The children jumped off the cuckoo's back. 'Thank you ever and ever so much!' they said earnestly. 'You *have* been good to us!'

'Not at all, not at all!' said the cuckoo. 'I've been delighted to have you. Now I must say goodbye and get back quickly or the giants will miss me.'

The children felt sad at parting with such a good friend. Mary kissed the cuckoo on her beak and tucked her red shawl under her wing for her to take back. The cuckoo's eyes were full of tears, for she had liked the two children very much indeed.

'Goodbye, my dears, goodbye,' she said. 'Take care of yourselves, and find that little Princess soon! Perhaps you will get her today!'

'Goodbye!' cried the children, and waved to the cuckoo as she rose into the air, her slippered feet tucked well under her, and a little bit of the red shawl hanging down from under her wing. They watched her until they could see her no longer.

Then they turned to look at the market-place. Now, the next thing to do was to find out where Sly-One the gnome lived!

CHAPTER SIX

In the Land of Storytellers

Long-eared gnomes were talking all around them. Nobody took the slightest notice of the two children. They went up to a tall gnome with a long beard and spoke to him.

'Good morning! Please could you tell us something?'

'Anything you like!' said the gnome at once, most politely.

'Could you tell us where the gnome Sly-One lives?' asked Peter.

'Certainly,' answered the long-bearded gnome. 'Do you see that big building over there, with the plants in tubs outside? Well, he lives there.'

'Does he?' said Peter doubtfully. 'It looks like a concert hall or something to me. Does he really live there?'

'Haven't I said so?' said the gnome, frowning so crossly that Peter started back in alarm.

'All right, all right!' said the boy, waving the gnome away. 'I believe you! Thanks very much!'

He took Mary's hand and they went to the big building. The great doors were open and they went inside. How strange! It certainly was exactly like a concert hall, for there were rows and rows of chairs there. There was a bent gnome sweeping the floor and Peter went up to him.

'Where can I find the gnome Sly-One?' he asked politely.

'Never heard of him,' said the old bent gnome, still sweeping.

'But he lives here!' said Peter.

'No, he doesn't,' said the gnome, sweeping so near Peter's feet that the boy had to jump out of the way. 'Can't you see this is a concert hall? Does it look as if anyone lived here? You're just playing tricks on me. Get away with you!'

He swept his big broom at Peter and over went the little boy, bump! He jumped up, glared angrily at the gnome and ran back to Mary.

'Sly-One doesn't live here,' he told her. 'What a storyteller that long-bearded gnome was in the market-place!'

'Well, come on,' said Mary, anxious to get out

of the dark, cold hall. 'We'll ask someone else.'

So they went out into the sunshine again and looked round. Standing in the middle of the road was a gnome policeman, his helmet shining brightly. They went up to him.

'Please could you tell us where the gnome Sly-One lives?' asked Peter.

'Yes,' said the policeman, and he pointed up the street. 'You want to walk up the hill there, and down the other side. Turn to the right at the baker's shop and you'll find it is a house with a bright yellow door.'

'Oh, thank you very much,' said Peter gratefully. He took Mary's hand and off they went up the hill.

'We should have asked that policeman before,' said Peter. 'Policemen always know!'

They reached the top of the hill and went down the other side. They came to a road that led off to the right and turned down it.

'Now we must look for a house with a yellow door,' said Peter.

So they began. The first door was a blue one. The next a green one, and the third one a black one. They went all down one side of the road, and then began on the other side.

And there wasn't a single house with a yellow door! Not one!

'That's strange!' said Peter, puzzled.

'Do you think the gnome's door *used* to be yellow and he's just had it painted another colour?' said Mary.

'Well, we'll ask,' said Peter. So he knocked at the nearest door, and when it was answered by a little gnome servant he asked her politely which door in the road had once been yellow.

'Oh, *all* the doors were yellow yesterday!' said the little servant-gnome with a giggle, and she slammed the door in Peter's face. He stood looking at it, red and angry. Mary pulled his arm.

'The people are all mad!' she said. But Peter suddenly knew better. Why hadn't he thought of it before?

'They're not mad!' he said. 'They're story-tellers! Aren't we in the Land of Storytellers? Well, we can't expect anyone to tell us the truth then!'

'Oh,' said Mary, dismayed. 'Of course! I hadn't thought of that! I suppose everyone will tell us untruths, no matter what we ask them.'

'So goodness knows how we shall find out where Sly-One lives,' groaned Peter. 'Look, Mary – there's a little seat by the roadside. Let's sit down and eat an apple each. If only, *only* we could find someone as nice as that cuckoo! She didn't mind what she did to help us.'

'There aren't many people like that,' said Mary wisely. They sat down on the seat and munched apples. A little boy-gnome ran up and stared at them. He held out his hand for a piece of apple. Peter suddenly thought of an idea. He took another red apple and held it out to the little gnome.

'You can have this if you'll tell me something,

84

little gnome,' said Peter. 'Where does Sly-One live?'

'He lives in the cave on the hillside yonder,' said the gnome, his eyes gleaming at the sight of the apple. He pointed to where a green hill rose. 'His cave has a round blue door with a big golden knocker on it. That's where old Sly-One lives.'

'Thank you,' said Peter, and he gave the gnome the apple. He ran off munching it.

'Well, it seems as if we've found out at last where Sly-One lives,' said Mary, finishing her apple. 'Come on, Peter, let's go up the hill.'

Off they went. The hill was steep, but a little winding path led upwards, and they followed it. They came to the cave and saw that it had a round blue door fitted into it. There was a bright golden knocker on the front. Peter was just about to knock when Mary saw a notice by the side of the door. She read it.

'The cave of Surly the Bad-Tempered Gnome,' she read. 'Don't ring or knock.'

'Look, Peter,' she said, in surprise. 'Whatever does this notice mean?'

Peter read it too, and then frowned. 'It means that that little boy-gnome has told us a story too,' he said gloomily. 'I shouldn't think Sly-One lives here – unless he lives with Surly! They would make a good pair!'

'Well – shall we knock and see?' said Mary. 'It says, "Don't knock or ring," but surely the knocker must be meant for knocking!'

Peter knocked loudly, for he was now feeling in a very bad temper. The knocker clanged on the door with a most surprising noise. A growl arose from inside, and then the children heard the clatter of quick, angry footsteps. The door was flung open and out came an ugly gnome with the most bad-tempered face that Peter had ever seen. He whirled his arms about and shouted angrily.

'Get away! Be off with you! Run along! Grr-rr-rr-rr!'

'You ought to be a dog!' said Peter, disgusted.

And then, to the children's enormous astonishment, the gnome at once changed into a big dog who ran at them, showing his teeth, and growling fiercely. Peter caught hold of Mary's hand and ran down the hill as fast as he could.

The gnome-dog stopped half-way down, changed into himself again and laughed loudly. Peter and Mary gazed at him and thought he was the most unpleasant person they had ever met.

'Why ever did you say he ought to be a dog?' said Mary. 'It was a dangerous thing to say!'

'Well, how was I to know he'd turn into a dog just because I said that!' said Peter, still feeling cross. 'I expect that horrid little gnome we gave an apple to thought it was a great joke to send us up to Surly's cave. Nasty little creature!'

'What shall we do now?' asked Mary, as they went on down the hill. 'We shall never find out where Sly-One lives at this rate!'

'*I* don't know what to do,' said Peter gloomily. 'We can't get sense or truth out of anyone here. I'm sorry for Fenella if she is living here, poor little girl!'

'Oh, Peter, we *must* think of something,' said

Mary. 'Oh – I know! Couldn't we find someone who doesn't belong to the Land of Storytellers? Then perhaps they would tell us the truth and we could find out what we want to know.'

'That's a good idea, Mary,' said Peter, cheering up at once. 'We ought to be able to see a pixie or a brownie who doesn't belong here but is just visiting. We'd better go back to the market-place. There are more people there.'

So back they went. The market-place was just

as crowded as ever – but, as far as the children could see, there was nobody there but gnomes, and they must belong to the Land of Story-tellers. They looked about everywhere for an odd pixie or a brownie, but not one could they see.

Then suddenly they saw a pedlar carrying a tray open in front of him. It was slung round his neck by a ribbon. The pedlar looked like a pixie and had a jolly, smiling face.

'Look!' said Mary. 'Let's ask *him*! I'm sure he's not a Storyteller.'

So Peter went up to the pedlar, who at once said, in a loud, singsong voice – 'Ribbons, buttons, cottons, silks, hooksaneyes, tapes, scissors, thimbles, ribbons, buttons, cottons, silks, hooksaneyes. . . .'

'You've said it all once!' said Peter. 'Wait, I want to ask you something!'

'Ribbons, buttons, cottons, silks,' began the pedlar again, but Peter wouldn't let him go on.

'STOP!' he shouted. 'Do you know where the gnome Sly-One lives?'

At once the pedlar turned pale and looked all round as if he were afraid of someone hearing what they said.

'Sly-One, did you say?' he said, in a whisper. 'Why do you want to know about *him*?'

'Because he has captured a great friend of ours, and we want to rescue her,' said Peter.

'Oh, I wouldn't go near that gnome, if I were you, really I wouldn't!' said the pedlar earnestly. 'He's very wicked and very powerful. He has turned lots of people into earwigs, slugs and snails.'

'Oh dear!' said Mary, who didn't like the sound of that at all.

'I don't care *what* Sly-One has done,' said Peter stoutly. 'We've just *got* to rescue poor little Fenella. Pedlar, we have asked ever so many people here where the gnome lives and they've all told us wrong. Can you tell us truthfully?'

'Oh, yes,' said the pedlar. 'I don't belong to the Land of Storytellers, you know, so I speak the truth. I wouldn't live here for anything! Why, the people can't even tell you the right time!'

'Well, where does the gnome live?' asked Peter.

'He lives in a very tall castle just on the borders of this country,' said the pedlar. 'It hasn't any doors at all, except one which disappears as soon as Sly-One has gone in or out.'

'Goodness! Then how shall we get in to rescue Fenella?' cried Mary in dismay.

'There are always the windows,' said the pedlar.

'Will you tell us how to get to the castle?' asked Peter.

'I'll come with you, if you like, and show you the way,' said the pedlar obligingly. The children were delighted to hear this. The pedlar made his way down the street with Peter and Mary behind him. As he went, he cried his wares.

'Ribbons, buttons, cottons, silks, hooksan-eyes, tapes, scissors, thimbles. . . .'

The children followed him through the town and out into the countryside beyond. When he had passed all the people he stopped calling out and beamed round at the children.

'My name's Pop-Off the Pedlar,' he said.

'What a strange name!' said Mary. 'Why are you called that?'

'Oh, well, I'm always popping off to different places, you know,' said the pedlar. 'What are *your* names?'

'I'm Peter, and my sister is Mary,' said Peter. 'Is that castle very far, Pop-Off? I'm getting rather hungry.'

The pedlar rummaged about under his silks and cottons and found a paper bag. He handed it to the children.

'There's enough lunch for us all there,' he said. Peter undid the bag. There were tomato sandwiches, slices of currant cake, and some sweets. It was a very nice lunch. They all munched joyfully as they walked along the dusty road. The hedges were white with may, and the cuckoos called loudly all around them. They reminded the children of the cuckoo-in-the-clock, and they did wish she could be with them.

After some time they passed round the foot of a high hill, and there, rising steeply on the further side, was a strange sort of castle. It was more like one great tower than a castle. It rose high up, almost into the clouds. As the children drew near they could see that there was no door at all and that the windows were set so high up it would be impossible to climb up to them.

'Is *that* where Sly-One lives?' asked Peter in dismay.

'It is,' said Pop-Off. 'If the Princess is there she will probably be in the very topmost room of the tower. That's where Sly-One keeps his prisoners.'

'Look!' said Peter suddenly, pointing up to the top of the tower. 'Do you see that handker-chief waving from the window up there, Mary? Surely that must belong to Fenella. Perhaps she has seen us coming!'

'Ribbons and cottons!' said Pop-Off, in excite-ment, 'that must be the little lady, sure enough! But how in the world are you going to get to her?'

The children walked all round the strange tower-like castle. It was impossible to find a door – and just as impossible to reach a window. If they couldn't get inside, how could they get Fenella out?

They sat down under a bush, so that if the gnome should come along, he would not see them. Then they all frowned and thought hard.

'If only we could borrow a ladder!' said Peter.

'Impossible!' said Pop-Off, at once. He was frowning so hard that the children couldn't see his eyes. Suddenly he leapt to his feet and did an excited sort of jig, crying, 'Ribbons and buttons! Buttons and ribbons! Of course, of course!'

'Pop-Off, whatever is the matter?' said Peter, in surprise. 'Do be quiet. The gnome might hear you!'

Pop-Off sat down in a hurry.

'Well, I've thought of a most marvellous plan,' he said. 'Really wonderful! I've a little friend, a brown sparrow that I once saved from a cat. It always comes to me when I whistle for it. It will help us to save Fenella!'

'Yes, but Pop-Off, how?' said Peter doubtfully.

'Look here!' said the excited pedlar, showing them the rolls of ribbons and tapes in his basket, 'I've got something here much better than a ladder! I've got strong ribbons and tapes that will make a fine rope, long enough and strong enough to rescue anyone!'

'But how will you get it up to that top window?' asked Peter.

'That's where my friend the sparrow comes in!' said Pop-Off gleefully. 'I'll give him a piece of ribbon to take in his beak, and it will be tied to a rope made of tape and ribbon below. He will fly up to the window with it and give it to the Princess. She will draw up the rope, tie it to her bed, or something, and let herself safely down! What do you think of that for a plan!'

'Splendid!' cried the children, delighted. Mary hugged Pop-Off joyfully. Really, what good friends they had found in their adventures!

'First we'll make the rope of ribbons and tapes,' said the pedlar. He quickly unrolled the ribbons and shook out the tapes. The children watched him beginning to plait a strong rope. He did it so quickly that they could hardly see what he was doing – but soon a plaited ribbon-rope began to coil round him as he worked. The children tried to help, but they could not work half so quickly as the excited pedlar, so they soon gave it up, and watched his clever hands weaving in and out.

'You've made miles, I should think!' said the children, at last.

'Well, we want a long rope to reach right up to that high window,' said the pedlar. He looked at the ribbon-rope round him. 'Still I think that's about enough. Now I'll whistle for my little friend!'

He put two fingers into his mouth and gave a long and trilling whistle, repeated three times. The children waited. For three minutes nothing happened – and then they saw a small speck hurtling through the air towards them. It was the little brown sparrow. It chirruped joyfully when it saw Pop-Off, flew on to his shoulder and lovingly pecked at his ear.

'Listen, Bright-eyes,' said Pop-Off to the waiting sparrow. 'I want your help. Do you see that window high up there, with the handkerchief waving from it? Well, I want you to take this little blue ribbon in your beak and fly up there with it. Give it to the person in the room, and she will know what to do with it.'

'Chirrup, chirrup!' said the sparrow, and at once took the end of the ribbon in its beak. It flew away and the children saw it mounting higher and higher towards the little window at the top of the castle, the blue ribbon fluttering out behind it. It flew right in at the window, and then flew out again, without the ribbon.

Someone inside began to haul up the ribbon swiftly, and the ribbon-rope, which was tied on a long way below the ribbon rose higher and higher up the tower walls. The children watched in excitement. Soon Fenella would appear and climb down to them! Dear little Fenella! It would be so lovely to see her again!

CHAPTER SEVEN

Sly-One the Gnome Again!

But Fenella didn't come. Nobody peeped out of the window. The ribbon-rope hung there, moving slightly in the wind. The children wondered what could be happening. Surely Fenella would know what to do?

'Oh, Peter, suppose she is tied up and can't get to the window!' said Mary suddenly. 'Or she may be ill in bed?'

'I didn't think of that,' said Peter, looking upset. 'Well, there's only one thing to do! I shall climb up the rope myself and see what has happened. I can manage to untie Fenella if she is bound, and then together we'll climb down again.'

The brave boy ran to the rope-end and soon began to swarm up. The castle wall was very rough indeed, and he found that he could climb up the wall with his feet and haul on the rope with his hands. It wasn't very difficult. Mary and Pop-Off watched him going higher and higher. At last he reached the topmost window and went in.

He looked round. There was no one there at all! The room was completely empty except for a strong wooden post to which the ribbon-rope was tied. Where was Fenella? Someone must have tied the rope there!

Just then Peter heard a chuckling laugh. He turned and saw, not Fenella, but Sly-One the gnome, coming in at the door! What a fright he got!

'So you thought you'd come and rescue the Princess, did you?' said the gnome. 'Well, she isn't here. I've put her somewhere else! Ho, ho, ho! And now I've got *you* as well!'

Peter ran to the window, meaning to climb down the rope, but the gnome stopped him.

'No, no!' he said. 'Let the others come too! I've been watching you all for some time. Quite a clever idea, this rope brought up by a sparrow. Oh, yes, quite clever! But not clever enough!'

The gnome went to the window and shouted loudly, 'Help! Help!'

Mary and Pop-Off heard, as he meant them to do. They thought it was Peter calling them. Without a moment's pause the two ran to the rope-end. They swarmed up the rope just as Peter had done, and, panting and puffing, reached the topmost window one below the other. The gnome reached out and hauled them in, then he stood and laughed until the tears ran down his wrinkled cheeks!

'You have walked so nicely into my trap!' he said, at last, grinning at the sulky children and the angry pedlar. 'Did you think you could rescue Fenella so easily? No, no, you are no match for a gnome like me!'

'Where is Fenella?' asked Peter fiercely.

'Well, seeing you are all going to stay here as my prisoners for some years to come, I don't see that it matters my telling you what you want to know!' said the gnome. 'She is hidden away in a deep cave under the Shining Hill, and the Goblin Dog is guarding her. Ha! ha! There's a fine piece of news for you! Think that over for a few hours!'

The horrid gnome walked out of the door and slammed it. They heard him slipping great bolts outside and turning a key in the big lock. They were prisoners! He had snipped the ribbon-rope, so that they could not escape out of the window – what in the world were they to do?

'This is dreadful,' said Peter, sitting down on the floor and putting his head in his hands. 'Just when we thought we were so near to Fenella! Now she is goodness knows where, and we are prisoners too!'

'I know where Shining Hill is,' said the pedlar gloomily, 'and I've heard of the Goblin Dog. We could never, never rescue Fenella from him. He can smell people from five miles away and he never sleeps. And, ribbons and buttons, how we are to get away from here I *don't* know!'

All that day the children and the pedlar stayed in the topmost room of the high castle. When evening came the gnome opened a sort of hatch in the great door and pushed through a tray on which were pieces of bread and a jug of water.

The three of them ate their miserable meal in silence. Then they once again wondered how they might escape. Pop-Off leaned out of the window and wondered if he could climb down the castle wall. But it was too dangerous to try.

'We can't get through that great door, and we can't get out of the window,' he groaned. 'It's impossible, quite impossible to escape. We must just make up our minds to stay here.'

The children agreed with him. It *was* impossible to escape. There were only two ways out of the room and neither way could they take. They lay down on the mattress all curled up together for warmth, and soon, tired out with their adventures, they fell asleep.

In the morning they awoke, feeling more hopeful – but as soon as they had once more looked out of the window and felt the strength of the great door they sighed again and knew that escape was out of the question. The gnome opened the hatch and pushed through a jug of milk and some bread and jam, but he said nothing at all. He seemed to be in a hurry.

The children and Pop-Off ate their breakfast

and looked as miserable as could be. If only they had something to *do!*

'If only we had some game to play!' said Mary. 'Haven't you any game of cards, or snakes and ladders in your tray, Pop-Off?

'No,' said Pop-Off. 'I only sell ribbons and buttons and things. Haven't you any marbles, Peter? Surely you may have some in your pocket?'

'I don't think so,' said Peter, feeling in the pockets of his shorts. He turned out everything he had there – a dirty handkerchief, a long piece of string, a squashed toffee, a pencil, a notebook – and a little round pillbox.

'What's in that box?' said Pop-Off.

'I've forgotten,' said Peter. He opened the box and stared at the fine purple powder inside, puzzled. Where could it have come from? He had quite forgotten. But Mary knew! She gave a loud scream of joy, and made Peter jump so much that he nearly spilt the powder.

'Peter! Peter! Don't you remember? It's the box of powder that our mother gave us! She said it might come in useful some day. Oh, Peter, perhaps it will save us!'

Peter's face brightened up. Of course! But how could the powder help them? He didn't know what it could do or was meant to do.

'Let me look at it,' said Pop-Off suddenly. He looked at the powder carefully and then smelt it. Then he tasted a tiny bit and quickly spat it out.

'I do believe – I – do believe –' he began in great excitement, 'it's Disappearing Powder!'

'Whatever do you mean?' asked the children, astonished.

'Wait a moment,' said the pedlar. He took up a little of the powder and spread it on to a silver thimble that he took from his tray. As the children watched they saw, to their amazement, that the thimble seemed to be crumbling away into thin fine powder, so fine that when Pop-Off blew it, it flew into smoke and disappeared before their eyes!

'There you are, I was right!' said Pop-Off, in the greatest delight. 'It *is* Disappearing Powder. It makes things disappear!'

'Well, shall we spread it over ourselves and make ourselves disappear, then?' said Mary.

'Of course not!' said Pop-Off scornfully. 'Whatever would be the use of that? We'd vanish completely and never come back!'

'Well – how can we use the powder to help us, then?' asked Peter.

'We'll rub it on the great door!' said Pop-Off, grinning joyfully. 'It will make it disappear – or any rate part of it will vanish, a big enough piece to make a hole for us to squeeze through. We'll be able to escape after all!'

The children stared at him, their eyes wide with amazement. Of course! How clever of Pop-Off to think of such a thing! What a good thing he happened to be there with them, for they themselves would never have thought that the powder could do a strange thing like that!

'We'll wait until the gnome has given us our midday meal,' said Pop-Off, planning hard. 'Then, when we think everything is safe we'll make a hole in the door with the purple powder, creep through it, run down the stairs and find a way of getting out of the Tower.'

'But there aren't any doors to it!' said Peter.

'Oh, never mind!' said Pop-Off. '*We'll* find a way, once we're out of this horrid little room!'

Peter put the box safely away in his pocket. Then they sat and waited patiently until Sly-One came with their dinner. He came at last, thrust a tray through the hatchway in the door, chuckled hoarsely to see their three pale faces, and disappeared.

On the tray were meat sandwiches, three slices of bread, and a big jug of water. The children and Pop-Off ate hungrily, and then looked excitedly at one another. Was it safe to try the powder?

'I should think we might try now,' said Pop-Off at last. He took the box from Peter, emptied a little of the powder into his hand and began to rub it on to a small piece of the door, rather low down. The children watched, excited. After a while that part of the door seemed to crumble away, and the three could quite well see through the hole it made! The pedlar blew hard and the crumbling piece flew into smoke.

Again Pop-Off rubbed more powder on to the next piece of the door and again the same thing happened. It crumbled away and a bigger hole still came!

'I do hope we have enough powder to make a hole big enough for us to squeeze through!' said Peter.

'Oh, plenty, I should think!' said Pop-Off, blowing away more of the crumbling wood into smoke. He went on with his work, and by the time he had used all the powder in the little round box there was a fine big hole in the door! Mary knew that she and Peter could easily squeeze through it, and she hoped that Pop-Off could too. He was bigger than they were.

'Now!' said Pop-Off at last. 'Let's get through! But mind! Not a scrap of noise! I'll get through first, and you two follow.'

He began to crawl through the hole. His tray stuck sideways and he took it off and gave it to Peter to hold. Then he managed to get right through easily. Peter tipped the tray up and just got it through the door, too. Pop-Off slipped it over his neck again.

Peter went next and then Mary. They stood outside the great door and looked round them in silence. They were on a small landing, set with doors like their own. Before them stretched a long, steep flight of stairs, thickly carpeted.

'Down we go!' whispered Pop-Off, and set off

down the stairs. The others followed. Down they went and down and down. Would the stairs never come to an end?

They passed many, many doors, all of which were shut. Strange noises came from behind some of them – whirrings and whinings, growlings and snortings. The children wondered what was in the rooms and hoped that none of the doors would open as they passed!

One door did swing open! Out of the room peeped a large cat with green whiskers. Its eyes opened wide as it saw the three creeping down the stairs. It was just going to mew loudly, when Pop-Off stepped up to it and raised his fist so fiercely that the cat, with a frightened squeak, shut the door quickly. Pop-Off saw a key in the lock and quick as thought he turned it and grinned at the others.

'He won't be able to give the alarm!' he whispered. 'He's safe there for a little while!'

On and on went the pedlar and the children, creeping silently down the endless stairs. And at last they came to a great hall, hung with curtains of all colours. Pop-Off held out his hand to stop the others and carefully peeped round the bend of the stairs to see if anyone was there.

Sly-One was sitting at the table, eating a good dinner!

Pop-Off stared in dismay. Now what were they to do? He took a look at the thick curtains that hung all round the hall. Perhaps they could hide behind those. He made the children understand, by nods and pointings, what his idea was.

Sly-One made a great deal of noise as he ate. He had very bad manners. Pop-Off thought this was a good thing as perhaps the noise he made would prevent him from hearing the children creeping behind the curtains. He slipped behind them first and then Mary followed him silently. Just as Peter was going too a reel of cotton fell from the pedlar's tray and dropped on the floor!

The gnome stopped eating and cocked his head on one side.

'What's that?' he said aloud. 'Did I drop something?' He looked on the floor, but could see nothing.

'Must have been a mouse!' he said, and went on with his dinner. Peter slipped behind the curtains too, and all three trembled and shook because of their narrow escape.

The gnome finished his dinner. He yawned widely, with his arms above his head.

'Now for a good long nap!' he said. He went to a couch and lay down, first taking off his pointed slippers. He covered himself with a rug and shut his eyes. In half a minute the children heard long snores, almost as loud as the giants had made two nights before!

'Now's our chance!' whispered Pop-Off, peeping out. 'We must see if there's a way to get out.'

'This hall is hung all the way round with curtains,' said Mary, looking about her. 'There doesn't seem to be any window at all, and certainly no doors.'

'Unless they are somewhere in the wall behind the curtains,' said Pop-Off. 'There might be secret, hidden doors there. After all, the gnome must get in and out of the castle *some* how!'

So, on tiptoe, the children felt all the way round the walls behind the great coloured curtains. They came right back to the place where they had started – but not a door was to be seen! It was most disappointing.

'We haven't any of that Disappearing Powder left, have we?' said Mary in a whisper. 'We could make a hole through the walls if we had.'

'There's not even a grain!' said Pop-Off. 'I used it all up, every bit.'

They stood behind the curtains and looked in dismay at one another. Whatever were they to do?

Then Mary's sharp eyes caught sight of something in the middle of the floor of the hall. It was a large trapdoor!

'Look!' she whispered in excitement. 'Isn't that a trapdoor? Couldn't we get through it and escape that way before the gnome wakes up?'

The others stared at the trapdoor. Yes – it certainly did look like a way of escape! How marvellous!

The gnome still snored steadily. Pop-Off thought that there would never be a better time to escape than now. 'We'll risk it!' he whispered. 'Now, not the slightest sound, remember!'

They left the shelter of the thick curtains and

112

tiptoed across to the trapdoor. There was a big ring to pull it up, and Pop-Off took hold of it. He tugged – and the trapdoor came up easily and lightly. It was plain that it was used very often!

Below there was a flight of steps, stretching down into the darkness. Pop-Off wondered how they would see. He saw a candle and a box of matches lying on the gnome's table and tiptoed up to get them. At least they would have a light!

Peter went through the trapdoor first and then Mary followed. Pop-Off was just climbing through too when the ribbon that tied his tray round his neck caught on a nail and the tray tipped up. A dozen reels and skeins fell through the trapdoor and bounced down the steps!

The gnome woke up at once and looked round. Pop-Off hurriedly untwisted the ribbon from the nail, took a frightened look at the astonished gnome and then lowered himself at top speed through the trapdoor. The gnome sprang up with a roar of rage and rushed over to him.

Pop-Off pulled the trapdoor to with a clang. He hung on to it underneath, feeling the gnome pulling for all he was worth. Then Peter lighted the candle and Pop-Off saw, to his great delight, that there were two strong bolts on the underneath of the trapdoor. He shot them at once and let go his hold on the bottom part of the door. The gnome could not open it now!

'Quick! We'd better go whilst we've got the chance!' he said to the children. 'The gnome may find some way of getting through. He's clever enough, goodness knows!'

Sly-One was beside himself with rage. The children could hear him dancing about on the trapdoor, shouting and yelling in his harsh voice.

'He's saying something about the Goblin Dog,' said Peter. 'It sounds as if he's saying that it will eat us.'

'Rubbish!' said Pop-Off. 'The Dog is in the Shining Hill, far away.'

The little candle gave them enough light to see by as they made their way down the steps and through a dark and winding passage. Sometimes the passage opened out into caves and then closed again into a narrow way between dark rocks. It was cold and damp – but at any rate they had escaped! That was something to be thankful for!

'This must lead somewhere,' said Pop-Off hopefully. 'Perhaps we shall come to a signpost or something soon, which will tell us where we are going.'

And after a while they did. The signpost stood in a cave and had two arms. One pointed back to where they had come from and said 'To Sly-One's Castle.'

The other one pointed forward. When the children read it, what a shock they got!

This is what it said – "To the Cave of the Goblin Dog!'

'Buttons and ribbons!' said Pop-Off, in the greatest dismay. 'Who would have thought of that! That's what the gnome was shouting about, I suppose – saying we would be eaten by the Goblin Dog!'

'There is no way but these two ways,' said Peter. 'Either we go back to Sly-One – or we go forward to the Goblin Dog. Whatever shall we do?'

'Well, we were going to the Shining Hill to find the Dog's Cave anyhow,' said Mary, 'so we might as well go on. Fenella's there.'

'That's true,' said Peter. 'But it doesn't sound very nice, somehow.'

'Come on!' said Pop-Off suddenly. 'We're out of the frying pan and into the fire, it seems to me – but we may as well make the best of it and be brave!'

So on into the darkness they went, lighted by the yellow flame of their little candle.

CHAPTER EIGHT

In the Shining Hill with the Goblin Dog

They went through caves and passages again, and were glad of their candle, for there was no light anywhere – but at last, when their candle was almost burnt right down and they were all feeling tired, they came to a curious cave.

The walls shone brightly and lighted up the way so that they could see without their candle. Glittering stones sparkled in the walls of the caves, and Peter and Mary gazed at them in wonder. Surely they must be very precious stones!

They went on through more and more caves, all lighted by the same shining in the walls, the shining of hundreds of brilliant stones. Peter stopped and tried to get some of the stones out of the walls.

'What do you want those for?' asked the pedlar impatiently.

'Well, I thought that they would make a lovely present for the Lady Rozabel, and if I take some for my father, he could sell them and become a rich man,' said Peter, busily prising the stones away from the walls. He put a few dozens into his pocket, pleased with his find. If ever they got home safely how rich he would be!

'This is a wonderful place,' said Mary, as they walked on, lighted by the glittering stones all round them.

'It must be the inside of the Shining Hill,' said Pop-Off. 'It shines like this on the outside, too, but no one dares to go near it, because the Goblin Dog lives there. He is such a fierce creature.'

'Poor Fenella! I hope she isn't too unhappy,' said Peter.

They went on and on – and then suddenly they stopped. A dreadful noise came to their ears! It was like the barking and yelping of a hundred dogs!

'That's the Goblin Dog,' said Pop-Off. 'He's smelt us already. My goodness, we'd better be careful!'

'How can we be careful?' said Mary. 'We've *got* to go on. We can't go back!'

'That's true,' said Pop-Off mournfully. He

went on again, on tiptoe, peeping round corners carefully, as if expecting the Dog to come round any moment. It was very frightening! At last they rounded a shining corner and came out into a huge cave, lighted from end to end by the brightly glittering stones – and there, in the middle of it, stood a great dog, his eyes glittering like the stones, his big ears pricked up, his long and snake-like tail lashing to and fro like a cat's.

He barked – and how he barked! It was really deafening. He showed his teeth and the children gazed in horror. How could they hope to get Fenella away from such a fierce creature!

'Where is Fenella?' shouted Peter bravely.

'What's that to do with you?' growled the Goblin Dog, lashing his tail all the more fiercely.

Peter looked all round. There was no sign of Fenella. Where could she be?

'We want the Princess Fenella!' he shouted to the dog. 'Tell us where she is at once!'

'I shan't and I won't!' barked the Dog, and he showed his teeth again.

'Better not get him into a temper,' whispered Pop-Off, who was feeling very nervous.

'Well, I *must* find out what has become of the Princess!' said Peter. 'You look after Mary,

118

Pop-Off. I'm going to show that Dog that I mean what I say!'

Without showing the least signs of fear Peter stalked right up to the Dog. He was almost knocked down by the lashing tail, but he folded his arms, looked the Goblin Dog straight in the eye and yelled at him:

'WHERE IS FENELLA?'

'Where *you* can't find her, or Sly-One either!' said the Dog angrily.

'But aren't you guarding her for Sly-One?' cried Peter in surprise.

'Never you mind what I'm doing!' said the Dog. 'If you don't turn round, all of you, and go back the way you came, I'll bite you!'

He certainly looked as if he would. But Peter did not stir. That made the Dog angry and he suddenly leapt at the small boy, who was knocked over before he could get out of the way. He shouted, and Pop-Off ran to the rescue. But the Dog stood over him, growling.

Then, to everyone's enormous surprise, a sweet, soft voice cried, 'Goblin Dog! What is all the noise about?'

'That's Fenella's voice!' cried Peter.

'And that's Peter's voice!' cried Fenella, and scrambling through a hole in the cave wall came the little Princess herself. She flung herself on

Mary and Peter and cried tears of joy. The
Goblin Dog stood watching in amazement.

'Oh, Goblin Dog!' said Fenella reproachfully,
'I do hope you didn't frighten my friends. They
have come to rescue me, I'm sure.'

'I thought they were enemies,' mumbled the
Dog, drooping his tail and ears, and looking
thoroughly ashamed of himself. 'I thought I was
protecting you. How did I know but what they
might be friends of Sly-One? They didn't say
who they were.'

Peter stared in amazement. Wasn't the Goblin
Dog keeping Fenella a prisoner for Sly-One,
then?

'I don't understand,' said the boy. 'Fenella, isn't the Dog keeping you prisoner?'

'He was at first,' said Fenella, 'but I soon found out that he was a kind-hearted creature, and we became friends. Then he said he would protect me if Sly-One came to fetch me. Isn't that right, Dog dear?'

The great creature put out his tongue and licked the little Princess gently.

'I love Fenella,' he said, in a yelping voice. 'She is the only person who has ever been kind to me, or hasn't thought me ugly. Sly-One has always kept me here in these caves, for he said I was too ugly to be seen outside. So I grew fierce and lonely and hated everyone.'

'You're *not* ugly!' said Fenella, stroking his rough coat. 'You're the dearest, kindest, beautifullest dog that ever was, and I'd like to take you home with me and let you live in a lovely kennel in the palace yard!'

The Goblin Dog lay down on his back and rolled over in delight. Pop-Off and the children were too astonished to say a word. No wonder the Dog had been so fierce when he thought they had come to take Fenella back to Sly-One!

Peter patted him. 'If you're Fenella's friend, you're ours too,' he said. 'We all like dogs, especially a good, kind dog like you. Can you

tell me how to get out of here without going
back through the gnome's castle?'

'Oh, do tell me all your adventures!' said
Fenella, pulling at Peter's arm, before the Dog
could say a word. 'Do tell me how you got here!
Oh, it's too wonderful to see you all again. I
have been so lonely and unhappy, first in that
horrid gnome's castle, and then down here in
these caves. I really don't know what I would
have done without my kind Goblin Dog!'

The Dog licked Fenella again and then gam-
bolled happily round the cave. It was full of
delight to have so many friends round it.

'Well, is there time to stop and tell our adventures?' said Peter doubtfully. 'Oughtn't we to try and escape whilst we can?'

'Oh, we've got the Goblin Dog to protect us now,' said Fenella. 'Come and see the little cave I've got all to myself here. I was just going to have my tea. You can all have some with me. That would be lovely!'

She scrambled through the hole in the cave wall once more and everyone followed her, the Goblin Dog nearly getting stuck in it, for he was so big. On the other side was a cosy cave, its walls hung with red curtains. A small bed stood on one side, and a table and some stools were here and there. A little stove was in one corner and a kettle was boiling there.

It was strange to have tea in a small cave in the heart of the Shining Mountain. Fenella poured out the tea, and put plenty of sugar into everybody's cup. There was bread and butter and jam and a big fruit cake.

Whilst they were eating, Peter, Mary and Pop-Off told Fenella and the Dog all the adventures they had had. How the princess squealed when she heard how they had escaped from the giants! How she opened her eyes when she listened to the tale of Peter climbing up the tower wall, helped by the ribbon-rope – only to find the gnome in the room where he had hoped to find the little Princess herself!

'I did tie my handkerchief to the window,' said Fenella. 'I hoped, if anyone came to rescue me, they would see it flying there and know that it was a signal. I suppose the gnome heard that you were on the way, and hid me here, then waited for you to come, the horrid thing!'

'We didn't guess that you would make friends with the Goblin Dog,' said Peter. 'We were dreadfully worried about you.'

'How could I help making friends with him!' said Fenella, patting the Dog on the head and giving him a very large slice of fruit cake which he swallowed at one gulp. 'He's a pet!'

'I like him too,' said Mary, and the Goblin Dog hung out his tongue at her and panted with delight. He had very large, soft brown eyes, and, though he certainly was a strange and ugly dog, there *was* something very likeable about him. Pop-Off wasn't quite sure of him, but Peter felt certain he was a good-hearted animal, who had only turned fierce and disagreeable because people had been unkind to him.

They were just finishing tea very happily together when the Goblin Dog suddenly leapt to his feet, barked madly and lashed his tail about violently. It hit the teapot and knocked it over so that it smashed to bits.

'Goblin Dog, what's the matter?' cried Fenella, in astonishment. 'Look what you've done! You've broken the teapot! Oh, what a mess!'

The Goblin Dog took no notice of Fenella at all. He just went on barking as if he had gone quite mad. His tail swished about more quickly than ever and the children got hurriedly out of its way, for it was strong enough to knock them over.

The Dog growled and showed his teeth, his eyes gleaming, looking towards the hole through which the children had scrambled. Everyone began to feel frightened. Whatever had happened to the Dog?

'Is it someone coming?' asked Pop-Off suddenly.

'It's Sly-One. I can smell him,' said the Dog, with a low, fierce growl. Everyone was startled. Sly-One! He must have found some way of opening the trapdoor and come down after all.

'What shall we do?' said Peter. 'Dog, is there any way of getting out of this mountain except through the caves that lead to Sly-One's tower?'

'There's one other way,' said the Dog. 'There is a deep-sunk well not far from this cave. It goes right down from the house on the top of the mountain, to far below where we are standing now, for water. There is a hole that enters the well, a good way above the water. If we can get there, and one of us could get to the top, he could let down the bucket and take us all up to the top, one by one.'

'Let's try that way, then,' said Pop-Off eagerly. He didn't at all want to face the gnome again.

'Come along then, quickly,' said the Dog. 'Sly-One is a good way away yet.'

He led the way. Through winding passages, as dark as night except for the glittering stones here and there in the rock, went all the five, hurrying as much as they could. The Dog went first, and Peter went last, looking back every now and again to make sure the gnome was not near.

'Here we are!' said the Dog at last. They crowded round a small hole in the cave wall and peered through it. Far down below they saw the gleam of inky-black water. Above them rose the rounded walls of the old well. By leaning right through the hole and looking upwards Pop-Off could see a little spot of daylight – the top of the well. That made him feel most excited. If only they could get into the open air again!

'How are we going to get up?' he said. 'There is no way, except by climbing.'

'Couldn't you whistle for your little sparrow friend again, and let him fly up with another ribbon-rope?' cried Peter.

Pop-Off shook his head very dolefully. 'No, that's no good,' he said. 'I used all my good ribbon for the other rope. I haven't nearly enough left now.'

Fenella looked at the Goblin Dog's feet. She knew that he had long, sharp claws, much more like a cat's than a dog's. She put her arm round his neck and spoke coaxingly to him.

'Goblin Dog, you are very clever, and you have claws like a cat. Couldn't you climb up the well yourself? You are such a wonderful dog that I am sure you could do anything!'

The Goblin Dog swelled with pride to hear Fenella speak to him like that. He shot out all his long, curved claws and put up his ears.

'I'll try, Princess dear,' he said, and licked her little pink nose. 'I'd do anything in the world for you! I'll try to get right up to the top, and then I'll let down the bucket for you and draw you up again.'

He scrambled through the hole and began to climb up the rough bricked sides of the well. The bricks were very rough and uneven and he

found foothold easily enough – but the bricks were old and, as his weight rested on them, some of them crumbled away and fell with a deep splash into the water far below.

The four left behind watched with beating hearts. Suppose the Dog fell? He would tumble far down to the water, and how would he get out? More bricks fell and every time the bits came hurtling down everyone thought the Dog was falling too.

But fortunately he had twenty strong claws to climb with, and as he was quite fearless, he didn't at all bother about what would happen if he fell. He just went on climbing. Soon he grew hot and tired, and Peter and the others could hear him panting and puffing as he struggled upwards towards the spot of light.

'I hope he gets to the top before the gnome comes,' said Peter nervously. 'It wouldn't be very nice to have the gnome capturing us again, without the Dog to protect us!'

Soon they couldn't hear anything of the Dog, for he was so far up the well. Pop-Off leaned out into the well shaft and said that he couldn't see the spot of light at the top. The Dog must be there!

Presently there came a clinking-clanking sound and to everyone's delight a big bucket came down the well! Pop-Off caught it as it swung down on its rope, and stopped it. The rope was tightened from above, where the Dog was holding it. He had climbed up quite safely and had let down the bucket!

'Good old Dog!' said Fenella. 'I knew he'd do it! I shall certainly have him for a pet when I get home again.'

'Come on, now,' said Pop-Off, impatient to get out of the dark heart of the mountain. 'Fenella and Mary first. There's room for you both!'

The two girls climbed in and pulled on the rope. Immediately the bucket began to rise up the well. Up and up it went, as the Dog wound the handle of the well – up and up, up and up. And at last, there it was at the top, and there was the Goblin Dog beaming all over his ugly face at them.

'You're a dear!' said Fenella. 'Now let the bucket down again for the others.'

Down it went. Pop-Off and Peter were impatiently awaiting it. Would it never come?

Pop-Off heard a sound in the caves behind them. He listened. It was the noise of running feet and panting breath. It could only be the gnome, looking for them all! His heart beat fast. He saw that Peter had heard too. They kept as quiet as mice. Oh, if only the bucket would come in time!

Nearer and nearer the sounds came. Pop-Off looked up the well. The bucket was coming down, thank goodness, but how slow it seemed. It arrived at last and Pop-Off pushed Peter into it. He was just climbing in himself when the gnome arrived, panting and breathless, yelling for the Goblin Dog!

'Goblin Dog! Where are you? What have you done with Fenella? Goblin Dog, come HERE!'

He caught sight of the hole in the cave, and saw Pop-Off's scared face turned to him as he settled himself in the bucket.

'Pull, Dog, pull!' yelled Pop-Off, hoping to goodness that the Dog would hear him. The bucket began to go up, swinging from side to side on the end of the rope. Sly-One poked his head through the hole and stared in amazement up the well. He had no idea of such a way of escape. He could hardly believe his eyes.

Then he began to shake his fist and shout angry things. Pop-Off, feeling safe, shouted back. This made the gnome so angry that he leaned too far through the hole and fell down into the well! Down, down, down, he went, and then splash, he was in the icy water! Pop-Off laughed till he cried, but Peter was scared.

'Can he get out?' he asked.

'Oh, yes!' said Pop-Off, wiping his tears
away. 'He can use some of the precious magic
he knows, and he'll do it quickly too, for he'll
want to be after us again, I've no doubt! He will
hope to catch us all before we get Fenella safely
home! Don't worry your head about *him*, Peter!'

CHAPTER NINE

An Exciting Escape

At the top of the well all the five looked at one another thankfully.

'Well, we've escaped,' said Pop-Off, wiping his forehead with a big red handkerchief.

'Thanks to the good old Goblin Dog!' said Fenella, giving him a hug, at which he was very pleased.

'Where exactly are we now?' asked Mary, looking round her. 'Look, there's a cottage over there. Let's go and ask where we are.'

They went up to the little cottage and knocked at the door. It opened – and oh dear, who should be there but the Green Wizard, Sly-One's best friend! The Goblin Dog knew him at once, and whispered to the others.

'Ah!' said the Green Wizard, smiling round. 'Pray come in!'

But nobody wanted to! They didn't trust the

Green Wizard – and he might ask them some very awkward questions! They were sure he had recognized Fenella.

'You must have a cup of tea with me,' said the Wizard. 'I shall be very much offended if you don't. And I'm not a very nice person then, you know. Come in, do – I'll put the kettle on.'

There didn't seem anything else to do. They went into the cottage in silence. The wizard took up a kettle, and then looked annoyed.

'No water!' he said. 'Pardon me a minute – I'll get some from the well! It won't take a minute to let down the bucket.'

He ran out of the cottage with the kettle and went over to the well.

'My goodness! Sly-One is still at the bottom!' said Pop-Off. 'He'll come up in the bucket!'

They all felt very worried. They stood and looked at the wizard winding the chain of the bucket. It must have reached the bottom of the well by now. Then he began to draw it up again – and dear me – it seemed as if it was very heavy indeed!

'Suppose Sly-One's in the bucket – what shall we do?' said Peter, in dismay.

'Run, of course!' said Mary.

'But we'll never out-run the gnome!' said Pop-Off.

'*I* know,' said Fenella. 'The Goblin Dog is big and strong enough to take us all on his back and run with us, aren't you, Dog?'

'Certainly,' said the Dog, willing to do anything for the little Princess. 'Look – the bucket is coming to the top now.'

They all watched – and, just as they had feared, the gnome Sly-One had climbed into the bucket and had come up with the water! He leapt out in a furious rage and began to talk to the wizard, who listened in the greatest amazement. Then he pointed towards his house and the gnome grinned in delight.

'He's told him we're here!' groaned Pop-Off. 'Come on everybody, we must run!'

They rushed out of the back door. One by one they climbed up on to the broad back of the Goblin Dog, held tight to his hairs, and off they went, at top speed.

The Green Wizard and Sly-One came running out of the back door in a fury, when they found that Fenella and the others had gone. They saw the Dog rushing away with all the rest on his back, and the gnome danced with rage. Then he and the wizard ran indoors.

'They're up to some mischief or other!' said Pop-Off, looking back. 'They'll be after us before long!'

On went the Dog, galloping on his four feet, and everyone clung tightly. He went very fast indeed and Mary thought that surely no one could ever catch them up!

'The gnome and the wizard are after us!' cried Pop-Off suddenly. 'They've got a cat from Giantland, bigger than a donkey, and they're tearing along at a fearful rate!'

It was quite true. The giant cat covered the ground tremendously fast, and Pop-Off began to think it would catch them up.

'Faster, faster!' he cried – and the Goblin

Dog galloped more furiously than ever. The children had hard work to keep on his back, and if Fenella hadn't discovered two hard knobbly things sticking out of the Dog's back, she would certainly have fallen off. She held on to the knobs, wondering whatever they were.

Then a dreadful thing happened! The Dog suddenly tumbled, gave a yelp of pain and began to limp.

'What's the matter?' cried Pop-Off.

'It's a thorn in my foot,' groaned the poor Goblin Dog, limping along on three legs.'

'Stop a minute and I'll get it out for you,' called Pop-Off. The Dog stopped and Pop-Off slipped off his back. The Dog held up his foot and Pop-Off saw a big thorn there. He took a pair of tweezers from his tray and pulled out the thorn. But alas, the Dog's foot was so sore that he could hardly put it to the ground!

Pop-Off gave a despairing look back at the giant cat, who was swiftly coming nearing with the yelling gnome and wizard on its back. Then Fenella called to him.

'Pop-Off! What are these lumps on the Dog's back?'

Pop-Off looked and gave a howl of joy. 'Goblin Dog! You've never grown your wings! All Goblin Dogs can do that! Grow them now, whilst I rub the knobs and say the magic words. Then you can fly!'

'I'd love to,' said the Dog, pleased. 'I've always wanted wings, but Sly-One never would let me grow them.'

Pop-Off began to rub the knobs and chanted a string of strange magic words as he did so. To the children's enormous surprise the knobs grew larger. Then they burst like flower buds and out of them unfolded great yellow wings covered with large blue spots and circles. It was marvellous! The Goblin Dog flapped them proudly.

'Quick, get on again!' he called. We shall be caught unless I get away now!'

They all scrambled on, horrified to see how near the gnome and the wizard were. Then up into the air rose the Goblin Dog, flapping his enormous yellow wings, and going along at a great rate. Pop-Off looked down and saw the gnome and the wizard looking up at them in dismay. Their giant cat could not fly!

But Sly-One was not so easily beaten. He clapped his hands seven times and called out some magic words. And hey presto, his giant cat grew four pairs of wings and rose up into the air! He could fly as well as the Goblin Dog!

'Quick, Goblin Dog, quick!' shouted Pop-

Off, and the Dog panted loudly as he flew. Peter looked down desperately. Oh to see the bright towers and spires of Fairyland!

Then he suddenly gave a loud shout. 'Look! Look! Can you see what I see? There, in the distance? It's Fairyland, it's Fairyland!'

'Home! Home!' shouted Fenella. 'Hurry, dear Goblin Dog, hurry. We'll soon be home.'

But the Goblin Dog was getting tired. He had a heavy load on his back, and his wings flapped more and more slowly. At last, as he was nearing Fairyland, he flew so slowly that Pop-Off was certain the Giant Cat would catch them up. Then a fine and unselfish idea came into his head.

'Goblin Dog, fly down to the ground and let me, Peter and Mary get off,' he said. 'Then you fly on to Fairyland with Fenella – you'll fly much more quickly then.'

At once the dog obeyed. Fenella cried and said no, she wouldn't go without them, but Peter was firm and set her safely on the Dog's back. Then up they went together, the Dog and Fenella, and Pop-Off was glad to see how much faster they flew now that the Dog had a lighter load.

He pulled the others under a bush, for the Giant Cat was passing over. The Cat circled overhead for a few minutes to find out if anything was to be seen – but as the three of them kept perfectly still, it soon flew off again after the dog and Fenella.

'Now we must make our way home again as fast as we can,' said Peter. 'Please come with us, Pop-Off. My mother will be so pleased to know you when she hears what a friend you have been.'

'Well, I'd like to see you safely back home,' said the pedlar. 'So I'll come.'

CHAPTER TEN

Everything Comes Right Again

Now down below in Fairyland there was great excitement, for many people had seen the Goblin Dog in the distance. They ran to tell Lord Rolland, and he at once gave orders that fairy archers were to shoot at the Dog and bring it down.

'Goblin Dogs are wicked creatures, who help bad witches and gnomes to do their evil deeds,' said Lord Rolland. 'We will catch this one and take it prisoner!'

So the archers took up their bows and arrows and shot at the coming Goblin Dog. He was astonished when he heard the whizz of arrows through the air – and poor thing, he did not know what to do! He did not dare to turn and go back, for if he did he would fly straight into the Giant Cat! No, he must fly through the cloud of arrows and see if he could bring the little Princess safely to earth!

So the brave dog flew on, yelping whenever a sharp arrow pierced his big wings. Fenella clasped her arms around him, sobbing, for she knew what was happening and was dreadfully afraid that her dear kind dog would be hurt. Just as the Dog was about to fly over the walls of Fairyland an arrow caught him at the root of his right wing and he fell, unable to fly. He flapped with his left wing and managed to reach the ground safely with Fenella, just outside the gates of Fairyland.

At once the golden gates were flung open and out rushed a crowd of fairies, meaning to drag in the Dog to Lord Rolland – but when they saw Fenella climbing off his back they shouted in wonder and amazement.

'Fenella! The little Princess! Fenella!'

They rushed to her, took her hands and began to pull her into Fairyland. Above them they suddenly heard the rush of wings and looking up, they saw the great Giant Cat with the angry gnome and wizard peering down from its back.

At once the archers set their arrows to their bows and sent a hundred whizzing up into the air! The Giant Cat gave a yell and turned back at once, in spite of the angry shouts of the wizard, who tried to make it fly down and take Fenella from the fairies. No, the Giant Cat had had quite enough. It flew off steadily, giving little squeals.

The archers shot their arrows after it. The wizard suddenly gave a shout and clapped his hand to his leg. Then the gnome gave a yell and clapped his hand to his nose. Both had been struck by arrows!

'Serves them right!' said Fenella, who was watching. 'Nasty, horrid things! They deserve it! That will teach them not to come back again!'

'Oh, Fenella, dear little Fenella, come quickly to the Lady Rozabel, your mother!' cried all the fairies, and they tugged at her hands and arms, and ran through the gates. She pulled back, looking towards the Goblin Dog, who lay panting, his hurt wing stretched out flat beside him.

'I must go back to the Goblin Dog and see if he is hurt,' she said.

'No, no, he is a dreadful, horrid creature!' cried all the little folk at once. 'Leave him! We will see to him. Look! Look! There is your mother!'

At the sight of her mother the Princess forgot all about the Goblin Dog and rushed to the

Lady Rozabel. She hugged her mother and cried happy tears all down her cheeks.

'Come and see your father!' said Lady Rozabel, who was weeping for joy too. 'He does not know you are here! Oh, Fenella, darling Fenella, to think you are really home again at last!'

Fenella cried with happiness to see her own home again. She was so tired that she could

hardly keep her eyes open, but she wanted to tell her mother all her adventures – and especially she wanted the Goblin Dog fetched into Fairyland. But the Lady Rozabel would not let her tell anything that night. 'You are so tired, Fenella darling,' she said. 'Come to bed. Tomorrow you shall say all you want to.'

'But my Goblin Dog,' murmured Fenella, her eyes almost closing.

'We will see to the Goblin Dog,' said Lord Rolland grimly. He had no idea that the Dog had helped Fenella so much. He thought that it had flown with her by command of that gnome who had followed on the Giant Cat. He kissed the little Princess and hurried out to give his orders.

In a trice the little folk surrounded the surprised Goblin Dog, who had been patiently awaiting Fenella to come and fetch him and bathe his wing. They tied him up tightly, and took him to prison, threatening him with all sorts of dreadful punishments. He didn't know *what* to think. He was very unhappy.

The little folk dragged him to a prison cell and locked him up there. He was thirsty and hungry, and his wing hurt him – but no one paid him any more attention. They all thought that he was a wicked Goblin Dog, servant of the gnome who had taken Fenella away. So there he was left, sad and lonely, all night long!

And what about Pop-Off, Peter and Mary? Well, as soon as the Giant Cat had flown off with the gnome and the wizard, they crawled out from under their bush and looked round.

'I know where we are!' cried Peter joyfully. 'We are not very far from our own home. Look, Mary, there's the shepherd's hut that our father often uses in wintertime!'

Gladly they turned towards the little valley in which their own cottage stood. Pop-Off walked with them, wondering if the Goblin Dog had got safely over the borders of Fairyland with Fenella. Suddenly he gave a shout, and pulled the others under a tree.

'The Giant Cat again!' he said. They looked up. Sure enough it was the flying Cat, carrying on its back a squealing gnome and wizard, one rubbing his nose and the other his leg.

'They're going back!' said Pop-Off, pleased. 'That means Fenella is safe. Oh, how lovely! Well, we'll see her tomorrow!'

They walked on, and in two hours' time they came to the valley where their cottage stood. Not far off stood the golden gates of Fairyland. Outside, to the children's enormous surprise, lay the Goblin Dog, his hurt wing outspread beside him! There was no sign of Fenella at all.

'What's happened?' cried Peter, staring. 'Why hasn't the Goblin Dog gone through the gates with Fenella? Oh look – here comes lots of the little folk! Perhaps they are going to cheer the Goblin Dog, and take him into Fairyland.'

But to the children's enormous surprise they saw the Goblin Dog being roughly handled by the little folk, and dragged through the gates, a prisoner!

'I won't have that!' shouted Peter, in a rage, and he rushed down the hill towards the gates, shouting 'Stop! Stop!'

But the fairies did not hear him. They dragged the Dog away and the gates shut. Peter and Mary ran up to them and battered on them until the gatekeeper looked out in surprise.

'Let us in, let us in, we want to see the Goblin Dog and Fenella!' shouted Peter. 'The Goblin Dog is our friend! You shouldn't treat him like that!'

When the gatekeeper saw that it was Peter and Mary, he refused to open the gate.

'Don't you know that Lord Rolland said you were never to come into Fairyland again?' he said indignantly. 'Of course I shan't open the gate! You are two wicked children, and if the Goblin Dog is a friend of yours then you ought to be in prison too! Why, he had got our little Princess on his back and was flying right over Fairyland with her! If you don't go away at once I'll have you put into prison too!'

'Come away,' said Pop-Off to the two children. 'Something's gone wrong. Lord Rolland isn't going to forgive you, and he's punishing the poor old Goblin Dog, even though he helped us so. I expect Fenella has forgotten all about us.'

Very sadly the three of them walked away from the shining gates. It was dreadful to think that Fenella had forgotten them – but what else could they think? If she allowed the poor Goblin Dog to be thrown into prison she must indeed have forgotten her friends!

'Come home with us,' said Peter, slipping his arm through Pop-Off's. The pedlar was looking very sad. '*We* shan't forget how you've helped us, Pop-Off.'

They came to their own home at last. They pushed open the door and looked in. How lovely it was to be home once more! Their Mother was still lying in bed – and their father was cooking something in a pot by the fire. When they saw the two children they cried out in delight!

Peter and Mary flew to their mother and hugged her tightly, and then hugged their father. Pop-Off stood shyly by the door, feeling rather left out. But Mary took him by the hand and led him to their mother.

'Mother, this is Pop-Off, the pedlar,' she said. 'He has been such a good friend to us and to Fenella, and without him we should never have got home safely again.'

Their mother smiled at Pop-Off and held out her hand to him. She thanked him and told him that he would always be welcome at their cottage.

'We are poor,' she said, 'but you may know that what we have we will always share with you, Pop-Off.'

'But we're *not* poor now!' said Peter gleefully. He remembered the shining stones he had taken from the walls of the caves under the hill, and he emptied them out of his pocket on to the kitchen table. His father stared at them in amazement.

'They are worth a fortune!' he said. 'Tell me how you got them!'

Then all their adventures were told, Peter, Mary and Pop-Off talking fast, first one and then the other. Their father sat amazed, handling the precious stones in wonder. Their mother lay listening, frightened when she heard of all the dangers they had passed.

'Well, we rescued Fenella, as we said we would!' said Peter. 'And we've made Father rich with these shining stones. We shall be able to leave this little cottage and take a nice house, just as you have always wanted, Mother!'

'The only thing we haven't been able to do is to make Mother well,' said Mary.

'But *I* can do that!' said Pop-Off unexpectedly. He rummaged through his tray and found a small yellow bottle. 'This is witch-medicine, powerful enough to cure anyone of any illness. Take three doses, Madam, and you will be cured!'

Well what do you think of that? Peter and Mary could hardly believe their eyes! Their mother took a dose at once and said she felt better immediately.

'You will be able to get up after the second dose, and after the third you will be cured!' said Pop-Off, glad to think that he had been able to bring such happiness into the little family.

'I *am* hungry!' said Mary suddenly. 'It seems ages since we had tea in the little cave under the Shining Hill.'

'Well, there is supper in the larder,' said her mother. 'Lay the table, dear, and we'll all have supper together. Then you three must really go to bed, for you look tired out.'

So they all had a happy supper together, and Pop-Off said that the rabbit pie was the best he had ever tasted! Then he curled up with Peter

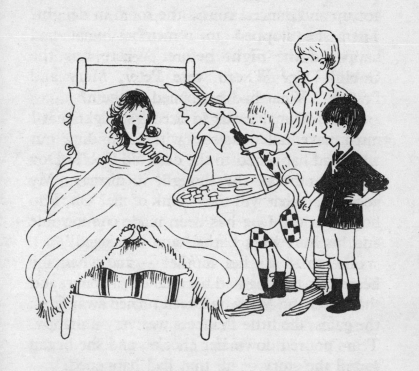

in his bed, and Mary went to hers. Soon they were fast asleep, and didn't even hear their parents talking about all the wonderful things they would do, as soon as they sold the shining stones.

The next morning was bright and shining. Away in the palace Fenella awoke in her own little white bed and wondered for a moment where she was. Then she remembered! How lovely, how lovely, she was at home again! She got up and danced round the room in delight. Then she stopped to remember what had happened the night before. Where was the Goblin Dog? Where were Peter, Mary and Pop-Off? What had happened to them?

'Oh, dear me, I was so tired last night that I must have fallen asleep without finding out what had happened to the dear old Goblin Dog and the others!' she thought in dismay. 'My goodness, what will they think of me? Oh, I do hope that the Dog has been made comfortable and his hurt wing bathed and bandaged!'

She ran to ask her mother – and when she heard that the dog had been taken prisoner, and that Peter and Mary had been turned away from the gates, the little Princess was very unhappy. Tears poured down her cheeks, and she began to tell the story of all that had happened.

'They are my best friends,' she sobbed. 'Peter and Mary rescued me, and the Goblin Dog was so kind and helpful. Oh, you shouldn't have put him in prison. He will be so unhappy!'

When her mother and father heard all that had happened, they were filled with astonishment. So Peter and Mary had *really* gone to rescue their little daughter – and the Goblin Dog was not wicked, but good and brave!

'This must be seen to,' said Lord Rolland at

once. 'We will get the Goblin Dog here and thank him.'

So, much to the Dog's surprise, he was taken from the prison to the palace – and there Fenella met him and flung her arms around his hairy neck. Lord Rolland and Lady Rozabel patted him and praised him, and very soon the court doctor had bound up his wing. He was given an enormous meal, and felt very happy indeed.

'And now, Mother and Father,' said Fenella

firmly, 'I want to ride on the Dog's back to Peter's home, and fetch him and Mary and Pop-Off back into Fairyland. And we are going to ride round all the streets so that the people can see us!'

Off she went, and soon the Goblin Dog arrived at the cottage in the valley. How delighted Peter, Mary and Pop-Off were to see him, and how they hugged Fenella!

'Jump on, all of you,' said the Princess beaming. 'We're all going back to Fairyland!'

'But will Peter and I be allowed in?' asked Mary doubtfully.

'Of course!' said Fenella. 'If they don't let you in, *I* won't go in either! I'll come and live with you!'

But, of course, they were all allowed in through the shining gates – and dear me, what a crowd of little folk there were, lining the streets and looking out of the windows to see them all pass by! How they cheered! You should have heard them!

'Three cheers for Fenella! Three cheers for Mary! Three cheers for Peter! Three cheers for Pop-Off! And three cheers for the good old Goblin Dog! Hip-hip-hurrah!'

Someone tied an enormous bow of red ribbon round the Goblin Dog's neck. He *was* so pleased! Then off to the palace they went and Fenella's father and mother helped them all off the Dog's broad back.

Lady Rozabel hugged Peter and Mary and thanked them very much for all they had done. She shook hands with Pop-Off, who blushed with pride.

'We'll have a big party in the palace garden this afternoon,' said Lord Rolland, smiling at everyone. 'Everybody shall come. And this evening we'll have fireworks!'

'Can the Goblin Dog sit next to me at tea-time?' asked Fenella anxiously. The Dog wagged his tail in the greatest delight.

'Of course!' said her father.

So that afternoon the Goblin Dog sat by Fenella, and Mary sat on her other side. Next to Mary and the Dog were Peter and Pop-Off, and next to Lady Rozabel and Lord Rolland were Peter's father and mother! Oh, it was a grand time!

'In return for the bravery and kindness of your children,' said Lord Rolland to Peter's father, 'I'm going to present you with a small castle not far from my palace, in Fairyland. And I shall hope that you will be good enough to allow your children to play with Fenella every day.'

Wasn't that lovely? How the children cheered!

'I shall be delighted to accept!' said Peter's father, bowing. He was very grand indeed in some fine clothes that he had bought with the money from the sale of the precious stones. 'I am a rich man now, thanks to the stones that Peter brought home, and I can well afford to live in a castle. My wife too, thanks to the pedlar's wonderful medicine, is quite cured of her illness.'

'Oh, Father, what about a reward for Pop-Off?' said Fenella. 'Could he come and live at the palace?'

'No, little Princess,' said Pop-Off, at once. 'I should not be happy living in one place. I am only happy when I am wandering about. But I will often come to visit you.'

'And we'll always buy all our ribbons, cottons, silks, tapes, buttons, hooksaneyes and everything from you!' said Fenella, hugging the blushing pedlar, who was really having the time of his life.

'What about the Goblin Dog? What shall his reward be?' asked Lady Rozabel, patting the happy Dog.

'*I'm* giving him his reward,' said Fenella, at once. 'I've already emptied my money-box, Mother, and I've given the money to Mister

Hammer, the pixie carpenter. He is making the Goblin Dog a most beautiful big kennel. And he's to live just outside my bedroom window and protect me all his life, because I love him so much!'

The Goblin Dog was so delighted that he cried big tears of joy into his dish of milk and biscuits. He couldn't ask for anything better than to look after the little Princess Fenella.

And now Peter and Mary live in their castle in Fairyland, and their mother and father are as grand as can be. They often see Pop-Off, and he always has tea with them and with Fenella when he visits them.

As for the Goblin Dog, you should see his kennel! It is painted a lovely blue, and every nail in it is made of gold. No wonder he is proud of it!

They all go for a ride on his broad back every Saturday afternoon for a treat, sitting between his great yellow wings – and you may be sure he *always* brings them back safe and sound!

Enid Blyton's Enchanted Tales

ADVENTURES IN FAIRYLAND

Nine enchanting tales from the land of
the weird and wonderful. A colourful
collection of stories about wicked
wizards, evil enchanters,
clever children and lots,
lots more!

£2.99
ISBN 0 09 940806 6

Enid Blyton's
Enchanted Tales

THE MAGICAL SHOP

Three green goblins, Tuppeny, Feefo and
Jinks, set up a little shop which sells
anything in the world to witches, fairies,
elves and gnomes. Soon, business picks up
and the goblins' magical adventures
through Fairyland begin...

£2.99
ISBN 0 09 941095 8